ANTE UP!

Vytamin Voyce

Cover designed by: Donna Osborn Clark

www.creationbydonna.com

Layout and Interior Designed by: Glenda A. Wallace

www.interiorbookdesigns.com

Editing: Laurie's Write Touch: www.laurieswritetouch.com

Published by: Vytamin Voyce

www.vytaminvoyce2.com

ISBN 978-0-615-56660-3

It has been a long road to walk down but, God has blessed me. To my Uncle Huck, Grandma Aloha Smith and mom, Linda Wiggins: Thank you all for inspiring me from above to write this novel. I miss you dearly, and I pray you rest in peace.

ACKNOWLEDGMENTS

First and foremost I would like to thank my Lord and Savior, Jesus Christ. I finally finished my first novel. YAY ME!!! I would like to send love to my dad and mom. Mom, oh how I wish you were here to celebrate this dream come true with me. I miss you and I LOVE YOU. (Tears) Second, I would be remiss if I did not thank my daughters, Shakiya Jeanette and A'Niyah Lynae, the absolute loves of my life. I live and strive for you every day. I must also thank my Aunts Lisa (Norval) Powell and Aloha (Leon) Oatman, and all of my uncles. Thank you to my best friends Buddha (Steve) Harper and Joe (Kena) Frisby, as well as my favorite cousins, Shaykina (William) Prince, Shantel Copeland and Ebony Palmer.

What would any of us be without friends who encourage us, push us, love us and give it to us straight? I am blessed to have many friends like that, and I must now thank my dear friends Kenyetta, Hope, Tasha, Tracey, Tracy, Vicki, Sherene, Mona, Evonne, Kenya, Kiyia, Stanelle, Shalyn, Jolena and Lamont Rohakemma, Nycole, Sherri, Shennita, Sandra and Dino, Meka, Raiketa, Carla, Kisha, Samantha and Rock, Keith, Angel and Iris, Ayanna, Denise, Malik, Iyanna, Janey, Mr. and Mrs. Bishop, Dallas, AB, Ms. Marilyn, Country, and Snowball.

I would also like to thank my former co-workers at Hilton: Gloria, Lisa,Valarie, Rosel, PJ, Maribel, Movita, Tita Baby, Mike, Craig, Jorge, Lance, Clarence, Chuck, Carl, Lykesia, Irene, Debbie, Ann, Sylia and Carol. I'd like to thank my co-workers at Caesar: Lisa, Larry, Monica and Ed, Larry, Jack, Robin, Sylvia, Angie, Trish, Tamia, Marisol, Shanda, CeeCee, Danise, Indra, Mike, George, Stephen, Corn and Adam.

I'd like to thank all of my Facebook friends. And I'd like to say a special thanks to V-Team (promoters), 456 productions (promo video), Donna (Rob) Clark (book design), Rosalyn Loatman (Web site design), Dave -DB Photography (photos) and Laurie D. Willis (editor).

Finally, I'd like to thank the following businesses and individuals: Iron Sharpens Iron, SJHB, Corrine's Soul Food, Pastor James (Angie) Clements and my True Praise Family.

I sincerely and humbly thank each and every one of you who have been part of my life. I am grateful we have crossed paths, and I am so blessed that many of you encouraged me to keep going no matter what.

Jesus I couldn't have done it without you.

Chapter 1

A DREAM COME TRUE
~MONDAY~

The sun is brightly beaming through the 15th-floor windows of Barker's office, which overlooks Philadelphia, The City of Brotherly Love. In fact, Barker had to pull the shades a little closer to each other to dim the sunlight, which is usually very shiny early in the morning. She walks around giving thanks to The Lord for another day and a gorgeous office. Then she wonders aloud *who would ever have thought that I, of all people, would have such a fancy office – and on the 15th floor no less?* As Barker spins in her chair she continues admiring her surroundings and congratulating herself. She also thanks God for her best friend and sister in Christ, Malaika, who has been by her side in good and bad times. Malaika always told her God would deliver her from any and all negativity. When she'd say it Barker didn't always believe it and now, in the prime of her life, she finds herself wondering, *can God really make my life better?* After a few seconds, Barker's thoughts shift to her office, which she acknowledges is uniquely decorated.

The office has a color scheme that probably wouldn't suit most people's tastes, which makes it easier for Barker to adjust to because she likes things that are different. You see, Barker is her own woman, and she beats to her own drums. Her office reflects her tastes and her tastes alone. Anyone walking in Barker's office expecting to find the same, boring furniture found in most offices would be highly disappointed, and that's just fine with her. The room is outlined in burgundy and cream, and a burgundy soft leather sofa and two oval tables rest in its center. The wall next to the door is adorned with many pictures of Barker's friends and family. On the other side of her office is a small dining table that seats two. Her very old-fashioned desk is extremely neat and clean, and a large calendar sits noticeably on top of it. Her desk nameplate reads L Janae Barker.

Janae Barker is fairly tall with smooth, cinnamon-brown skin. If you glance at her chances are she'll remind you of Gabrielle Union and Angela Bassett simultaneously. That's because Barker's as cute as a button but also well-toned. Her taste in clothes is impeccable, but she tends to let the occasion dictate what she wears. She expresses versatility when coordinating outfits, but for the most part when teaching class she prefers dressing comfortably.

Because of all the frustration and constant attacks she endured from the enemy while working in casinos, Barker decided to inform wannabe dealers about "that life." Even though the enemy tries to deter her from doing The Lord's will, Barker has peace in her life. Her peace abides in the knowledge that in the midst of her darkest hour God showed up and showed out for her. Barker doesn't necessarily understand why He chose to save her, especially when she was living in a different world, but she's so grateful He did.

Barker presses the intercom to learn whether her class of wannabe dealers has arrived. "Mona, how big is the class?" Barker asks her secretary. "Ten people and I already reminded them class runs Monday through Friday from 10 a.m. to 1 p.m.," Mona's voice floats back through the intercom as Barker smiles broadly with anticipation.

Barker checks herself again to ensure she's legit and comfortable before beginning her journey. She's wearing a DKNY gray sweat suit with matching gray and white Nikes. She has a tight wardrobe with the latest fashions. In fact, walk into her bedroom closet and you'd swear you're in a Saks Fifth Avenue store. But Barker knows right now it's not about her clothes or her jewelry. Right now it's not even about her. It's about being honest with her students and telling them exactly what they need to hear. She hopes and prays her students are ready to hear what goes on in the casino business, because she's prepared to tell them the truth, the whole truth and nothing but the truth so help her God. She will tell them the excruciating truth about working in the casino and how it tore apart her life. She will also tell them how her life was saved. After all, if He can do it for her, He can and will do it for them.

Barker bends down to pick up her briefcase and grab her BlackBerry off her clean, organized desk. Just before walking out of her office she steps back to inspect her hair one last time in the full-length mirror hanging behind her door. The building she works in is 30 stories high, and the employees who occupy it push different agendas. Many retirees teach classes on what they did in the casino industry. Occasionally, Barker sits in on their classes but never hears anything new. Former cocktail waitresses complain about players who constantly order drinks but don't tip. Once in one of those classes Barker thought about her life as a dealer and muttered under her breath, "Sometimes players didn't tip me either."

Barker walks to the opposite end of the hall, taking at least one minute to reach the elevator doors leading downstairs to her 8th-floor classroom. Every morning she passes her personal receptionist, Mona, and four other receptionists.

"Good morning, Ms. B," Tasha said.

"Good morning, Tasha."

"Good Morning, Ms. Barker," said Nakia.

"Good Morning, Nakia. How is your son?"

"Good, thanks."

"Good day, Barkerrrrrr," Linda said, purposefully dragging out her name.

"Good Morning, Lindaaaaa," Barker replied, dragging out Linda's name just as long.

Barker greets these four women daily, but this particular morning as she walks past the last receptionist she notices the woman's head down on her desk. "You're not speaking on this blessed morning, Barbara?" Barker asks, interrupting her dozing. "Oh good morning. I'm still tired from last night." Barker is itching to tell Barbara the job she's doing isn't worth the trouble, but she thinks like any other Ms. Know-it-All she must find out for herself. Even so, Barker can't resist saying a little something to Barbara. "Remember I said you need to leave that casino alone," she says in a firm, yet loving tone. Even though you're only a part-time dealer it still wears you down." Barbara looked up at Barker long enough to say "I know, I know" before lying her head back down on her empty desk.

God give me strength, Barker thinks to herself as she enters her classroom. There are only three guys in the room. Usually there are more guys than girls. Okay, *God, lead me so I can help the lost. Anyone who works in the casino or wants to work in the industry is lost,* she continues thinking to herself. *Once I was lost but now I'm found.* Whenever she starts a new class, Barker asks God to guide her in the right direction. After her few moments of meditation, she walks into the classroom and greets her students with warmth, happiness and a big smile.

"Good morning, class. My name is Ms. Barker, Ms. B. or Ms. Janae," Barker said. "Everyone calls me Ms. B, but call me whatever you prefer. I'm easy." The class greets her back with a hearty "good morning." Barker tells them she wants to pray before getting started. A few students are rolling their eyes, some are chewing gum and one still has on his earphones. Barker ignores the misconduct until her prayer is over. "Lord

heavenly father, I thank you for another day and for my class.
I ask you to protect my spirit while teaching. I reverently ask
this prayer in Jesus' name. Amen." Only a few students echo
amen, but that doesn't bother her one tiny bit. She figures by
week's end everybody will be saying amen – or at least she
hopes they will.

"Let's get started," Barker says politely. "I want all
earphones off, chewing gum in the trash can and please, no
attitudes. It will make our week run more smoothly. Anyone
that needs to go to the bathroom, feel free to go. I'll remain
silent until you're all back in the room. It's a must that everyone knows what's about to happen in their future. You can
take notes, but no recording please. I'll be passing papers
around for you to supply just a little bit of information,
including your name and why you want to be a dealer. Drop
the information slips in the bin located in the back of the class
at the end of this session. Thank you."

As Barker sits in the front of the classroom she feels a bit of
anxiety. The students are also a tad anxious, determined to
learn as much as they can about the casino industry. Barker
proceeds to explain she decided to teach these classes to
enlighten them on what to expect if they become dealers. Her
reason is simple: She knows they're unsuspecting of the
stresses and frustration they'll endure if they enter the casino
industry without the proper mindset. Barker knows all too
well that a strong frame of mind is necessary to comprehend
and deal with the sickness that goes on in the industry. The
casino is like a continuous motion picture – only the ending is
usually negative.

"My first name begins with an L," Barker begins. "I'll never tell anyone my first name because the whole time I worked
in the industry my name was called more than 50 times a day,
five days a week for 10 long years. We dealers had to wear
name tags displaying our first name at all times. Needless to
say, everyone called my name constantly, including managers,
co-workers and players. You know how a 3-year-old repeated-

ly says 'mommy, mommy, mommy?' That's how my name was said over and over and over all day everyday for 10 long years. Sometimes it still rings in my ears." Barker scopes out her students, who appear very impressed by what she's saying.

"I started working in the industry when I was 24," she continued. "One of my childhood friends, Stony, used to be a dealer. I saw one of her checks, and it blew my mind! To me it looked like she'd hit the jackpot. Stony was clearing $850 in only four days, and that was all I needed to see. From that point I was determined to become a dealer making that fast money. And just think. All I had to do was attend training school for two months to learn the games. Hmmm. That was right up my alley."

Barker caught her breath for a millisecond before continuing.

"By 27 I still had no real family ties, meaning I had no children," she said. "I'd been working in the industry three years; I'd moved out of the hood, was sporting a brand-new Lexus, had money in the bank and was eating whatever I wanted whenever I wanted." After that last comment Barker paused because she felt a need to expound on it. "I know how it feels not to be able to eat something you really want because you can't afford it," ... "So when I got in a position to eat whatever I wanted whenever I wanted, to me that was a big accomplishment."

Suddenly, Barker hung her head toward the floor as she realized the class had become as dull as watching paint dry. As she continued speaking she rose from her seat to try to bring some life and excitement back into the class.

"On my first day in the casino I realized with all of the hustle and bustle and slot machines it sounded like a game room, perhaps *Dave & Buster's* and *Chuck E. Cheese* all in one. The noise from the slot machines and the music they played was virtually nonstop.

The casino is decorated in bright colors, with bright lights, ugly tri-colored carpet and big dull windows. There are no clocks, not even one, so you never know what time it is. Trust me when I tell you some poor souls arrived at the casino around 11 a.m. and before they knew it, it was 11 p.m. No joke.

I had to wear dark blue pants, a yellow shirt, black sneakers and my name tag every single day. I worked eight-hour shifts, five days a week, and I always worked Friday, Saturday and Sunday because the casino seemed to be extremely busy on the weekends.

Class, I'm trying to remember everything I learned in training school, so please bear with me. I had to learn five games in two months – lickety-split. At one window I was learning, at the next window I was dealing. It was crazy. And everything was moving at a head-spinning pace. I felt so nervous and out of sync on my first day. I can remember that day just like it was yesterday. Mind you I still won't disclose my first name, the name I grew to hate."

Joe was my very first supervisor. "My name is Joe, and I'm your supervisor for today," he said as we met. "I'll be walking around showing you the ropes so you can know what to do around here. So, how many games do you have?" he asked. I looked at Joe with a slight smirk on my face and facetiously said, "I didn't bring any games, sir." Joe chuckled then said he meant to ask how many games I'd learned in training school. I flashed him a fake smile, told him five games and then named them: craps, blackjack, baccarat, roulette and poker. Joe told me I'd learned all the major games and management would love that because they could assign me all around the floor wherever they needed me. At the time I was a bit confused, but I played along and Joe was none the wiser. He showed me all the different sections of the casino floor, which is comprised of one row of games with four to eight tables each."

"Here's area one, all blackjack tables," Joe said while pointing. "I looked over the whole floor and noticed it was

covered with sections. At the top of each section identifying
numbers were written in bold. Interestingly, a quick glance at
the dealers' faces told me none of them was happy. For the
first two hours Joe gave me a tour of the front and back of the
casino. The front of the casino is for the customers. The back of
the casino is for employees only."

Barker did a long stretch in the middle of the classroom
then told her students she and Joe eventually stopped walking
as they approached a particular woman. "Kyna, this is L," Joe
said. "L, this is my wife, Kyna. She'll be showing you the
ropes until I come back from my break." As Joe walked off,
Kyna looked at Barker, told her it was nice to meet her and
began walking. "Let me take you to the café," Kyna said. "You
can eat all you want as long as you're on the clock." Barker
told her students how her heart nearly skipped a beat when
she heard she could eat for free – as long as she was on the
clock. She also told them she started calculating how many
times she'd get to eat and figured out that as a dealer she'd get
up to five breaks a day during an eight-hour shift.

"Class, I thought I was in Heaven when Ms. Kyna told me
that, but little did I know I'd be in hell real soon."

As Barker was thinking about all the food she could eat,
Kyna interrupted her pleasant thoughts by cautioning her to
be on guard at all times. "I don't know why you're in this
industry, but watch out for everyone because they're all liars,
cheats, gossips, complainers and will stab you in the back in a
second." Barker's smile quickly eroded, and in a matter of
seconds she was frowning and feeling as though she'd just
been burned.

"All jokes aside, L, I wish I'd never gotten into this industry," Kyna continued. "If I could rewind the clock 12 years I
would. Joe and I got in way too deep. The money was coming
fast, and we saw it as a way to put our children through
college and also pay off our debts. Everybody in here makes it
sound and look good, which is ironic considering 90% of them
don't even want to work here. Management doesn't care about

us. They care only about how much money we can bring in for the company. Their pockets are getting fatter and fatter, and our souls are getting thinner. L, use good judgment and ask God to guide you while you're working here. Anytime you need to talk I'm here for you." Kyna covered a lot of ground in a short span, but eventually Barker fully understood what her supervisor's wife was trying to convey. Kyna made it sound as though a person's life could be destroyed by the casino if that person allowed it. The women exchanged phone numbers, and Barker waited patiently until Joe returned so she could start her day on the floor.

Barker began walking around passing out papers and pens as she continued discussing the beginning of her experience with the casino life.

"Come on L, give me blackjack," Barker said, recalling some of the common phrases from players. "Bust mon-key...monkey. Now here I was, dealing for the first time to six players on a blackjack table and they're all screaming for me to bust the hand, meaning go over 21. I had 15 showing and I needed a seven or higher to bust the hand. Shoot, at first my naive butt thought they were calling me a monkey until Joe explained that a face card is called monkey and that's one of the favorite sayings from Asian players. Irene, a dealer stand-ing behind me, whispered in my ear, 'Good job, L, for this to be your first time.' Then Irene tapped me on my shoulder signaling it was time for her to resume dealing. I turned to Joe who also said I did great. It was pretty much the same routine all day. I got tapped on and off games. There were a few games I didn't know, but I had to tap on anyway and Joe walked me through them. He told me not to worry about the games I wasn't familiar with because I would catch on fast. At every game there was at least one player screaming for me to lose. Spit was flying from some of the players' mouths, and some of them had very bad breath. I just kept imagining Stony's check and thinking that mine would be a duplicate. L got to do what L got to do. That was my attitude at that time in my life."

While Barker was getting oriented, Joe told her it looked as though she was going to be one of the better dealers at the casino. Barker thanked him while faking a smile.

As Barker spoke, her students looked as though they were in a trance. Truth is, they were listening so intently – as if she was about to announce they'd all hit the lottery – they didn't realize how their faces looked.

"Class, are you paying attention?" Barker asked while jumping off her desk so she could walk around the room.

"Yes!" one student shouted emphatically.

"Go ahead. Tell us more," another eager student blurted out.

So Barker continued.

"I was so excited to get back to work the next day and have my own table for eight hours. I also looked forward to my 20-minute breaks. In the casino industry it's the law for us to get a break every hour so we can regroup physically and mentally. I thought it was great. I'd work five days a week, get one break every hour, get paid every week and I could eat for free. However, there truly was a price to pay for all of that…

Barker started clapping her hands to awaken the sleepy heads in the back of the room.

"That's it for today," she said. "We'll pick up tomorrow and I'll discuss the later years of my life as a dealer."

"That's it?" one student asked dejectedly.

"Yes," Barker replied. "I don't want to exhaust you with too much information all at once. You'll get restless, and I know you guys are hungry. Three hours are enough for one day. But I'll tell you what. We have 20 minutes left in class so I'll take questions from any of you that have them and answer them to the best of my ability."

The students all perked up.

"Who's first?" Barker asked.

The students all raised their hands, much to Barker's surprise.

"Okay. Since everyone has a question I'll go in order. Please state your name when I point to you and ask your question. And only one question per person, please."

"My name is Troy, and I want to know if you get a pension?"

"Good question," Barker said. "No. We get something called a 42k. You have to put your money in stock and pray you make money off of it. They save it until it's time for you to retire, and if you decide to take it out early you get penalized. They also allow you to borrow from yourself, and you must pay yourself back in installments. Next."

"James is my name. Do you miss the casino?"

"I miss my co-workers and all the laughs we used to have, but as far as the casino itself God is my witness I'm glad to be out."

"Next," Barker pointed.

"Lesa is my name. Did players ever harm you?"

"No, not me personally, but a few of my co-workers encountered players spitting in their faces, drinks being thrown at them and verbal threats. I will say it can be a dangerous industry because you never know what customers are thinking after they lose all of their money."

"Next," Barker said while pointing toward the sleepy head in the back.

"My name is Ebony. Why did you stay in the business for so long?"

"Good question, Ebony. My darling, once you're used to making that fast money and paying off a lot of unnecessary bills you get caught up thinking you can catch up. But it wasn't as easy as I thought."

"My name is Kiyia. Can you describe your last day with one word?"

Barker froze for a second as if she was about to relive her last day. Then she shouted, "Deliverance!"

Shane wanted to know how it felt to be instructing the class.

"It feels good. I feel grateful and blessed. Once a month I teach a class that reminds me how good it is to be out of the devil's palace."

"Next."

"My name is Tyree. Why did you call it the devil's palace?

"It offers drinks, gambling and parties to anyone over 21. You can get hooked on that type of life when you indulge in it year after year."

Barker notices a young lady who looks like she has it altogether. She's well dressed in a navy blue dress suit, and a briefcase rests on the side of her desk. As she rose she accidentally kicked her briefcase over.

"I have a statement and not a question," she said. "My name is Helen. I just want to thank you for teaching this class. My mom and dad both worked for the casino, and I watched the industry destroy them. My father is in jail for trying to rob the casino, and my mother turned to drugs after they laid her off after 25 years of service. My mother always said there's no job security in this industry."

"My, my, my. I'm totally blown away by your testimony," Barker said. "If you witnessed firsthand how the casino destroyed your family, why on Earth do you want to become a dealer?" she asked, raising her eyebrows.

"Oh no, not me, Ms. B," Helen quickly replied. "I just wanted more knowledge of the casino industry. I'm in law school because I want to try to get my father out of jail." As she spoke, Helen's pride was apparent.

Barker told Helen she was astonished by her thirst to learn more information. She could see in Helen's brown eyes just how much she cared about her family.

"God will work everything out in your favor, and if you haven't seen the movie 'Conviction,' rent it."

"Thanks," Helen said with a smile while picking up her briefcase.

ANTE UP! 13

"You're next," Barker pointed to the honey-skinned lady in glasses.

"Tundra is my name, and I want to know have you ever gotten sick because of a customer?"

"Good question. No I haven't, at least not that I know of. However one of my co-workers, Chilly, did. She was out for two weeks because she touched chips that were handled by a player with sores all over his hands and subsequently developed an itchy rash. There are a lot of germs being passed back and forth on gaming tables."

"Next!" Barker eyeballed the student.

"I heard they just blow smoke in your face and you're not allowed to say or do anything. Is that true?"

"That's true in a way. Some supervisors will ask them to blow their smoke in the opposite direction of your game. By the way, you never mentioned your name,"

"Oh, my name is Sherrie. Excuse me."

"It's ok Sherri. We just all need to know each other's names."

Barker began expressing the depth of her feelings with the group. She told them she cried many times. She cried to get out. She cried because she wanted to fight players and co-workers, including her supervisors. She told them so many people got on her nerves all the time. Barker shook her head in disgust as she listened to what she was saying, which took her right back to that awful place. Barker told her students she knew she had to break free from the casino industry before she ended up in a penitentiary.

"Although I cried a lot, I really cried once I got out, but those were tears of joy. My last few years of dealing were the worst. Now don't get me wrong. Working in the casino had its advantages as well. If you really needed a day off and you didn't rub anyone the wrong way, they granted it to you as long it wasn't a weekend day. But if you made requesting days off a habit, denial, as in your request was denied, became your best friend."

Barker walked to the back of the room as she began wrapping up her class. She told them about the time she tried to visit the casino after she'd quit and how management had her escorted off the property with a warning to never return. You see, she's banned from the casino, which means she can never work at or step foot on their property again.

"Do you have a class after this?" Shane asked.

"No, Shane. But in this building all different types of classes on casino life are taught. For example, if you wanted to be a room attendant, line servant, cashier or valet you could take a class about it. And the list goes on. These classes are just to inform you about casino life so you can have a better understanding of the in's and out's of what you're getting into and know the real deal. Too many of the workers make it look good on the outside, but they're hurting on the inside and wish they were doing what they want to do instead of what they feel they have to. I once was a victim of that."

Barker stopped talking and rubbed her head in relief as she thought about how good it felt not to be a dealer anymore – not to be trapped.

"Excuse me, Ms. B. Are you busy?" Barker looks back at Mona as she walks toward the open classroom door.

"Don't you see I'm on my way back to my office?" Barker questioned sarcastically. "No, Mona. I'm not busy. How can I help you?

"I'd like to know if I can leave early this afternoon." Just before Barker can answer her, Mona hands Barker her daily planner which was open to that day's appointments.

"All your messages are on your desk, and your favorite lunch is on your table," Mona said excitedly, assuming that would win Barker over and guarantee she'd get to take off early.

"Well thank you, Lord. I couldn't have prayed for a better receptionist," Barker said. "Yes, you can leave. Have a blessed afternoon, Mona."

"Thanks! See you in the morning," Mona shouted as she ran toward the elevators.

Once Barker reached her office she glanced over at the Chicken Caesar salad with a can of Pepsi next to it. Instead of eating first she decided writing in her journal, which she tried to do every day. After writing her last sentence she began reading her memos. Her mother had called. *Let me guess. She wants to borrow some money, because that's 'bout the only time she dials my digits.* Her best friend, Malaika, called also. Barker decided she'd return Malaika call once she got home. As Barker drenched her salad in Caesar dressing she thought about how very pleased she was over her first day with the new class.

WHAT DREAMS ARE MADE OF
~TUESDAY~

B arker wanted to get started quickly today. She had so much to tell her students about the players she dealt with in the past so she went straight to the point without holding anything back.

"Today we'll be talking about customers, which we also call players. Now I'm going to be doing some jumping around because there's so much to cover in a week's time. Barker's hands were on her hips as if she was speaking to her own children. Her tone was deliberate, and her expression is stern. She needed her students to understand the importance of what she was saying. "I know you all heard that ridiculous statement customers are always right. Well, they're not. As dealers we come across all types of players, including cheats, thieves, stinks, flirters, demanders, commanders, drunks, etc. You name it, and I've seen it or heard about it in different casinos. You can't even imagine all the things we went through as dealers. The one thing I disliked most was people used God's name in vain. All day long players screamed for God to help them to win money. They said stuff like 'Jesus help me,' or 'Lord have mercy,' or 'Mary and Joseph,' or 'Oh my God let me be a winner,' or 'I need a savior, holy hell,' or 'I have faith in you,' referring to us dealers. They'd also tell us they needed an angel or, when they hit, they'd been obedient and gone to church on Sunday so they knew they would win. I heard Jesus' name in the casino more than I *ever* heard it in church."

Barker told the students it didn't matter what game she dealt. Players intermittently called on God. She told them how she always thought God had nothing to do with the casino and certainly didn't condone gambling, which was a sin, but as a dealer she knew enough not to say anything. "A dealer's opinion didn't matter, so I just kept it all to myself," "The only thing that mattered was if a dealer had legs and arms – legs to walk back and forth to the gambling tables and arms to deal the cards." Barker thought at least one student might laugh at her joke, but none did.

"Yeah, all they do is call on The Lord with nothing on their minds but greed," she continued. "Ninety percent of the players worship us as the best dealers when they win, but if and when they lose we're the worst dealers they ever had. You have to be careful because those players will switch up on you in the blink of an eye. I tried to stay neutral. I never said too much. I just dealt the game I was assigned. Despite all the mess I saw and what I had to take from so many people I just kept it all inside. Usually I went home with migraines every day."

Barker held her head as if she was experiencing a headache that very moment. Then she continued lecturing.

"The players used to bang on the table demanding I lose. Can you imagine if I banged on your desk every two minutes for eight hours a day while music was playing and shouting was happening all at once?" she asked. "Trust me. There's an Advil just waiting to be popped from all that commotion. I dealt with players that picked their noses right in front of my face. After picking their noses they literally put their fingers in their mouths and then had the nerve to touch chips and pass the money with their un-sanitized hands. I used to be so upset, but unfortunately I needed the job and didn't have a formal education that would allow me to do anything else that could bring in the type of money I was earning at the casino, so that was what I had to settle for."

Barker put her head down shamefully as she continued speaking.

"Sometimes you could still see spit stains on the money. Oh, and let me not forget about the players who picked their teeth with a toothpick right at the table. I was just itching for some spit to hit my body so I could let them have it. One time a woman's nose was bleeding and she refused to get up from my table to handle her business. I called my supervisor, Alice, and she came over and made the woman leave my table. In fact, she lied and told the woman she couldn't come back to my table, but the truth is as long as the woman left and cleaned up her nose she could have come back to my table. But do you guys see how bad it gets? I'm telling you, when someone has a gambling problem it's hard to remove him or her from the table. There could be a fire in the casino, or someone could have a massive heart attack right there at one of the tables and players won't leave until someone makes them move."

Barker asked whether anyone needed a break and was pleased no one said yes. In fact, several of the students screamed "More, more." *Hmmm. I guess they really are paying attention to what I'm saying because they want to know the real deal about casino life. Well, at least they're listening.* After her thoughts, Barker smiled and continued, hardly skipping a beat.

"One player had sores all over his arms and hands, but I still had to deal to him. I'm telling you I was so mad. Another time a lady regurgitated all over the table, so we had to shut down the game, clean it up as quickly as we could and reopen. After the game reopened guess who was first person to sit down? If you guessed the lady who had thrown up, the one with the stinking breath, you're right. The industry is a really tough business to work in," Barker said while holding her nose for a quick second as if she still smelled the lady's foul breath.

"Players used to cough directly in my face, forcing me to tell them to cover their mouths. It's a shame because of course they were old enough to know their mouths should have been covered. It was as though I was a parent to people older than me."

Barker went on to tell them how people just didn't care about themselves. Once they walked through the industry doors, it was as though they were in a trance. So many players came to the casino in wheelchairs, dragging oxygen tanks, with tubes coming from their noses or on crutches. In some cases they were fresh out the hospital, and it looked as though they were trying to gamble because they foolishly thought money could win back their health. Needless to say it was a very depressing sight.

Barker recalled a time when Rosa, her co-worker, had a drink thrown in her face while Barker dealt Black-jack on the next table over. Rosa couldn't do or say anything if she wanted to keep her job. She just had to suck it up as the player ran off; however, she was given the rest of the day off with pay.

Barker also shared an incident that didn't seem fair to the dealers. One time two guys came to the table where her co-worker, Sherene, was dealing, and one of them threw $40 in ones on the table. Just as Sherene counted the last dollar the guys each grabbed one purple chip, totaling $1,000, and scrambled. The guys never got caught, however Sherene got fired because no matter what the chips were supposed to be guarded at all times.

Barker stood from her desk and asked, again, whether anyone needed a break before she continued. The entire class shouted *"MORE,"* only this time in unison and with more enthusiasm.

"You had to watch players at all times," especially the high rollers because they were so demanding. They came in stating what they wanted and talked to you any 'ole kind of way.

Most of the supervisors tolerated their crap because the high rollers spent so much money.

The industry catered to people that had money, and all we got were headaches, backaches and mistreated. I'm telling you this because it's important you understand and I really hope you're all listening. Don't get me wrong. Not all players were a pain in the butt. I'd say 70% of them had some type of issue they were dealing with, that they brought to the table. As a dealer I experienced at least 30 mood swings a day and had to hold them all in. That's why I went home with so many headaches."

Barker tried to paint a clear picture of how she was treated in the industry. In fact she wanted her students to *"feel"* her experiences as a dealer as much as they possibly could.

"I worked for tips, but I received them only when players wanted to tip because we weren't allowed to ask for them. Dealers made $4 per hour. I don't believe you heard me. Dealers make $4 *per hour*. That's right. We were paid a mere 16 quarters per hour. After 10 years I was making $6.50 per hour. Now you tell me who raked in all of the big bucks? It sure wasn't us dealers. After 10 years of experience I was making only $2.50 more than I made when I started. Something was definitely wrong with that picture. The casino was like restaurants. You had your fancy ones and your trashy ones. If you were in a fancy casino your tips were much greater than if you were in a trashy casino." Barker stretched her long arms and proceeded.

"I had to deal to so many people a day depending on what game I was on and how fast they lost," she said. "Just as fast as one player got up another player sat down. The games were like revolving doors. They kept going and going. Players stayed at the casino three to four days at a time, sometimes even weeks. Many of them wouldn't even change their attire. They'd just walk around looking lost and pitiful. This was what gambling did to people. It caused them to stop caring about themselves and their families. Those same poor, lost souls often asked my opinion on whether they were going to win or lose before they played on my table. I just used to say it is what it is. What I really wanted to say was I'm not a damn psychic. Players always looked to blame others for their losses, as if someone put a gun to their heads and made them gamble. They couldn't cope to the fact that it was their fault for stepping foot inside the casino in the first place."

Barker announced that since she had only 10 students she was going to wrap her lecture and allow them to ask questions, just as she'd done on the first day of class. Inside, she was excited to hear what questions they had for her today.

"Have you ever thought about stealing since you worked around so much money?" James asked.

"Yes. As a matter of fact it crossed my mind a couple of times," she answered. "It was never worth it, though. I heard about plenty of dealers from all different casinos getting arrested for theft. One dealer kept stuffing chips, or casino tokens, down his sleeve until a player informed his supervisor. The dealer was terminated right on the spot. The casino had so many eyes, so I just figured why steal and go to jail when I couldn't make any money from a prison cell.

"Were you ever involved with anyone you worked with, like a boyfriend?" Helen asked.

"No, not me personally, but I saw a lot of that going on, especially among married people. It seemed as though they came to work just to cheat on their spouse with their co-workers, or to flirt. During my days as a dealer men didn't have anything but dirty mouths, and every time a woman passed by their necks got stiff." Barker spat.

"Can you explain why you think the casino used you?" Shane asked.

"For the most part dealers were on the front lines of the casino and took all of the abuse from players and supervisors. Not to mention we dealt with germs, smoke and inconsideration. There was a *NO SMOKING* policy throughout the whole building, except on the casino floor. Smoking was even allowed around pregnant dealers. Upper management got the big bonuses, and no smoke was blown in their faces. They didn't have to deal with any attitudes, and I guarantee you they got every weekend off to spend time with their family. But I knew that was the price I had to pay for choosing that business. That's why I decided to teach this class, so you could hear the real deal and make an educated decision on whether to work in the casino industry, so you could make a reasonable choice. Next."

"Did you see a lot of bums?" asked Sherrie.

"I wouldn't necessarily call human beings bums. Less fortunate maybe," Barker said. "Yes, some players gave money to less fortunate folks, but most players wanted them removed from the areas in which they were playing."

Barker peeked out the gigantic, clear window overlooking Philly. *How delightful this was not to be looking out the dull windows of a casino* she thought before the next question.

"Did you see couples gambling?" asked Troy.

"I saw women with their boyfriends or husbands all the time, and some of them looked like they didn't want to be there," Barker said. "It was very disturbing to see a player trying to entice his companion to gamble. What a bad habit to force on someone."

"Did you used to see call girls?" asked Ebony.

"That's a nice way to say hookers. Yes. My heart bled even for them because they could have done so much better if they had just applied their time and talents. Those girls came into the casino trying to pick up men for money and ended up picking up diseases or drama. If they had picked up *Jesus* they wouldn't have had to worry about money because He would have provided all of their needs. But believe me when I say my co-workers, both male *and* female if you know what I mean, enjoyed staring at the women..."

Tyree stood, stretched his arms and then held them in front of him in a circle. "Did you see any pregnant women?" he asked as he sat back down.

"Now that was a truly heartbreaking site to witness – pregnant women gambling in the casino. I often wondered if they knew babies felt and heard everything their mothers felt and heard. When they were stressed from losing their money their babies were stressed, too. I also wanted to say something to them about sitting in all that smoke but I didn't. I just smiled and continued dealing. And since we're on the topic of parenting, let me tell you many parents left their children in the hallways, their cars and even casino hotel suites for many hours. As long as they were able to gamble they did. Next."

"Did your body ever hurt?" Lesa asked.

"My arms, legs, feet, head and every muscle in my body ached," Barker quickly said. "My back still hurts from time to time from all of the bending I did over the crap tables. Next."

"How many supervisors did you have? Tundra asked.

"I had a lot of supervisors, at least two or three a day," Barker answered. "Overall there were too many to count because we all had different supervisors daily. You never really knew to whom you were assigned until you actually got to your table. Along with the different supervisors came different rules and attitudes. Some supervisors didn't care what we did as long as we did our jobs correctly. Then we had the supervisors that thought they owned the casino and wanted to be all down our throats making us feel uncomfortable for eight hours. What a pain in the neck they were! I had to get with some of them on several occasions and let them know I wasn't the one. See, supervisors would try to take advantage of the ones they knew they could. I stood strong and firm. They knew not to try that bull crap with me. I just tried to do my job for the most part."

Barker shut the curtains and opened the classroom door. She inhaled and let out a sigh of relief because day two was over.

"Okay, students. That's it for today," Barker said. "If you think you heard some good stuff today just wait. I have some things to tell you that will blow your mind. I'm excited to share my experience with you, but before we exit I'd like to give God the highest praise so let's pray."

"Father, I apologize for not praying at the beginning of class, and I thank you for another blessed day. Please protect us, watch over us and give us traveling mercies in Jesus' name I pray. Amen."

Mona was hesitant to meet Barker by the eighth-floor elevators. As she re-read Barker's plans for the rest of the week she knew she'd told Barker's supervisors what she had planned for class on Friday – and that they were in an office waiting on her now. Mona gave Barker her pen and notepad for the unannounced meeting.

"What's the meeting about?" Barker asked Mona with an uneasy feeling. *Hmmm. I believe she told them something about the videotape. Oh Lord. Am I about to get fired right now?*

"Oh, umm" Mona stuttered, sounding very sympathetic. "The meeting is about you and the videotape." Mona didn't want to convey the message but to stay employed she had to do her job. Barker pushed the button to the sixth floor where the meeting was being held, instead of pushing the 15th floor where her office was located. Mona swiftly walked in the opposite direction as the chrome elevator doors closed. As she rode, Barker hung her head in defeat.

"Well.... well... well... how are you Ms. Barker?" Tony asked. Tony Coop is a white, short guy with a huge head. He had been Barker's supervisor the entire five years she was employed at *RBC*. Tony was very satisfied with Barker's work but knew what she was determined to show her class was a disaster. He didn't believe Barker was able or prepared to watch the videotape. Thanks to Mona's forewarning, Tony called an emergency meeting with his team members.

"I'm fine, but before you continue if you don't mind me asking, who are those two people?" Barker said with a very concerned look on her face while trying to see if she recognized them. They were all sitting at a round table with water and nuts in a silver dish placed in front of each of them. They all wore expressions as if Barker had lost her best friend, which made Barker more furious than curious.

What is my nurse Evonne doing here? I haven't seen her since my last appointment. Barker didn't feel comfortable having a meeting with her boss, her nurse and two strangers. Tony motioned for Barker to join them at the table. "I called this meeting today with your nurse, Ms. Evonne, Dr. Keith and Ms. Tracey," Tony said, "because I understand you're attempting to review the videotape again only this time with your class."

"That's right!" Barker said as she jumped from the table, accidentally tipping over a glass of water.

"Calm down Ms. Barker," Dr. Keith said while grabbing some paper towels and wiping the table.

"Excuse me. Who are you telling to calm down?" Barker asked angrily. "Don't you have some patients to drug?"

"Ms. Barker, I know you don't understand, but it's in your best interest not to watch the videotape," Ms. Tracey said.

"Okay lady. I was waiting for you to interrupt," Barker retorted. "Who are you and why are you all up in my business? See now I'm really mad. Mona called all of you about me wanting to view the videotape, huh?"

"Hold up. I rebuke that spirit right now in the name of Jesus," Ms. Tracey said. "Listen here baby girl. Where I come from we respect our elders. If you don't want me to go Madea on you, you'd better tone it down because I have no problem doing so. Now I came to this meeting to help talk some sense into you since I'm on the videotape as well."

"Oh, I'm sorry Ms. Tracey or is it Mrs. Tracey?" Barker asked, feeling ashamed over her emotional outburst. *Ms. Tracey could pass for a Madea look-alike,* she thought.

"It's just Tracey. I'm widowed."

"I'm just so tired of everyone trying to stop me from watching the videotape," Barker pleaded.

"Ms. Barker, we don't think you're mentally ready to watch this tape," Evonne whispered to her. "You might not be able to handle what you see."

"No disrespect to anyone, Mr. Tony, but am I'm fired?" Barker asked.

"Oh no, Barker. You're one of my best employees," Tony quickly said.

"Fine," Barker shot back. "You all have a nice day."

As she quickly stomped out of the meeting, angry thoughts of indignation swirled in her mind. *Who do they think they are telling me I'm not ready to watch the videotape? God has me. I've been praying for this to happen, and I need to get it done and over with.*

"Nurse Evonne, I'd like you and Dr. Keith to be on standby Friday from 10 a.m. to whatever time the class is over," Tony said. "I'll have a room next door set up for both of you to relax in while all of this takes place. Let's not forget that Ms. Barker lost her memory due to her severe headaches."

"You got it! I'll be right here," Dr. Keith assured Tony. "I'll have my assistant, Breon, handle all of my patients."

"Yup I'll be right here too," Evonne said with a slightly sinister laugh. "Your pay is much better than the pay at the rehabilitation center anyway."

"Ok. That's it for today. I'll see you all at the end of the week no later than 9:50 a.m. sharp including you too, Ms. Tracey," Tony said. "We might need some back up."

When *it* happened, the thing Barker can't remember, Ms. Tracey had to put her in a headlock. Ms. Tracey was one security guard you never wanted to make angry.

MY DREAMS
~WEDNESDAY~

B arker arrived at her office a little earlier than usual this morning. She wanted to write in her journal and talk with God before any of her co-workers arrived. Barker didn't know it, but a lot of people were praying for her speedy recovery. She thought watching the videotape would help solve unanswered questions. But who knew what state of mind it would put her in? She picked up her journal and wrote: *I couldn't believe yesterday. Everyone was making such a big deal over this videotape. What could possibly be on it? Is there something on it that I haven't already discussed with my students? The only thing they're going to find out is my first name, and I believe it's time to get over that anyway. The devil is a liar, and I should want to be called by my first name anyhow. That casino doesn't rule me.* After she finished writing, Barker closed her black and white journal. She reached across her desk and pressed the intercom for Mona, who she figured would be in by now.

"Mona, please come into my office. Thank you." Barker realized she forgot to pray, so she bowed her head and spoke quickly before Mona could interrupt. *Father God, thank you for this blessed day. And can you please place it on everyone's heart to leave me alone? Tell them Lord that I'm fine in the name of Jesus. Amen.*

"Mona, can you explain to me who those people were at the meeting yesterday?" Barker exploded. "Ahh... Ahh, I don't know all of them, Ms. B. All I know is supposedly they were all on the videotape," Mona stuttered. "I met nurse Evonne once when she dropped your meds off here at the office."

"Nurse Evonne helped take care of me with my best friend, Malaika," Barker told Mona. "Ok. It really doesn't matter to me. I really don't have much to say to you this morning anyhow. Everyone is starting to treat me like a baby that needs a hug. I know you know Ms. Tracey and Dr. Keith as well. I just want to be set free." Barker yelled and slammed her hand on her wooden desk.

"No more babyish pity stuff. Got it Mona?" Barker shouted. "I got it, Ms. B," Mona said as she bowed her head and left Barker's office.

Barker began thinking about what to tell her students in class. She really didn't want to trash the industry anymore than she already had, but decided she might as well finish what she started and continue keeping it real for her students' sakes. She knew the industry dumped on her for years and thought nothing of it. All she was to them was 86892, the number printed on her ID badge. Barker knew she could go on and on about the industry, so she decided to pick whatever came to mind and ignore what she'd already planned in her syllabus. After settling on the day's game plan, she noticed three bright red lines flashing on her intercom. "Mona, who's burning up my lines so early this morning? It's only 9:30."

"Your best friend, Malaika, is on line one. Mr. Tony is on line two. And Ms. Tracey is on line three," Mona said.

"Put Mr. Tony through and after him put Malaika through, but take a message from that Madea lady," Barker instructed.

"Good Morning, Mr. Tony."

"Well good morning to you, Ms. Barker. I just want you to know you're doing a fine job her at the *Rebuild Yourself Center.* This year you have the highest percentage rate of adult students who decided to go back to school to follow their dreams instead of working in the casino, and I just want to say congratulations."

"Thanks Mr. Tony," Barker said, smiling.

"People need to know the real deal about the industry because it'll eat you up and spit you out if you're not prepared for it," Tony continued. "I often wondered why they don't offer pre-training classes to inform people of all the jive they'll encounter on a daily basis, but I guess they don't want to discourage prospective employees. Well, have a good day."

"You too and thanks again," Barker said, gladly disconnecting the line. She wondered whether Mr. Tony was being sincere or disingenuous about wishing they offered pre-training classes, a thought that quickly disappeared as soon as she picked up Malaika's call.

"Yes, yes my love, my dear friend how can I help you this morning?" Barker asked with happiness.

"Good morning. You're so cheerful this morning," Malaika stated.

"Yes, God is good. I received the highest percentage rate this year once again and you know what that means. I'm moving on up like the Jeffersons, and I get a $10,000 bonus that I'm going to share with you."

"Great, Janae. Spend it wisely. You know I'm good. I just want to remind you that we want to pray with you tonight after Steve and I get in from the movies. We're going to see 'Not Easily Broken.' "

Barker's mood suddenly changed.

"Whatever you say. I guess Mona told you, too huh?" Barker was very disturbed that Mona relayed her business not only to her boss but also took it a step further and told Malaika.

"I love you Janae," Malaika whispered through the phone.

"Ditto. Now hang up my line." Barker hit the end button on her phone then pushed down hard on the flashing yellow light.

"What is it now, Mona?" Barker asked in an irritated tone. "Your students are all here waiting on you in the classroom," Mona responded in a low, almost scared voice. Barker glanced at her antique Oak grandfather clock. She didn't realize it was already a little past 10.

"Ok. Thank you." Barker reached for her briefcase as she double-checked her gear in the mirror. She was wearing a dark brown and cream Sean John sweat suit with high top cream Nikes. Her jet black curly hair was pulled back in a pony tail, a style she had a tendency of wearing due to comfort.

"Good morning Linda, Tasha and Nakia," Barker said as she passed by. "Mona, please remember to set up the class-room before you leave."

Linda, Tasha, and Nakia said good morning in unison.

"Ok. Will do! Enjoy the rest of your day," Mona said while sighing to herself. She knew Barker was upset with her, but she also knew she did what she did out of love and concern for her boss, not to belittle her or put people in her business.

Barker felt so good she skipped down the hall singing and thanking God for her achievements. *That bonus is going to do me justice.*

"Good morning class," Barker said, pausing to catch her breath.

"Ms. B., why are you huffing and puffing?" Kiyia asked with concern.

"I took the steps here. I'm feeling good this morning." Barker realized she wasn't young like she used to be. Back in the day when she played sports like soccer, softball and volleyball Barker never would have been winded after taking a flight of stairs. The entire class chuckled at her for being out of breath so early in the morning. Then Ebony raised her chestnut hand.

"Yes Ebony?" Barker said while closing the classroom door.

"Can I pray this morning?" she asked with nervousness.

"Yes Ebony. Why not." Inside, Barker's spirit was shouting. *Pray my child. Pray.*

Ebony's voice sounded sweet, clear and secure. "Heavenly father, I just ask you to touch us and allow us to get through life in a positive way and watch over Ms. B. and her class." Everyone said amen as Barker shouted Glory to God. She thought it was very kind of Ebony to want to pray and reminded her to always end her prayers by saying in Jesus' name, amen.

"I'm sorry Ms. B," Ebony replied.

Barker told her there was no need to be sorry. She just wanted her to know how important it was to seal her prayers in Jesus' name. *This is why I'm here to teach you, not only about the industry but also about my God,* Barker thought to herself. She truly believed it was her job to help the students understand about the woes of the casino business and the joys of God.

Barker smiled as she looked at her class. Everyone appeared to be focused and bubbly this morning. She told them class would be abbreviated because of her plan to show them the videotape on Friday. She stressed how important it was for them to be on time for Friday's class and told them the videotape she wanted them to watch was very touching. She never got the chance to finish watching it because at one point she froze and Dr. Keith and Ms. Tracey, who weighs every bit of 200 pounds, rescued her. Due to the circumstances, she hoped everyone would understand how important it was to view the videotape. Barker believed in her heart she could overcome her fear and finish the tape this time once and for all – with the help of her best class ever.

Barker repeated Tuesday's format, allowing students to ask questions before she spoke.

"We should be leaving around 12 o' clock so let's begin quickly," she said. Barker was kind of nervous because she didn't know everything that was on the tape. She felt as though she wasn't herself anymore, as if there was a fire burning inside that she needed to put out. Her mind, body and soul were screaming for freedom. She wanted to see the videotape, and her students wanted to see it, too. She knew because she overheard a few of them mumbling about it before she entered class. "What do you think is on that tape?" she heard Tyree ask Kiyia. Kiyia hunched her diminutive shoulders, trying to belie how much she cared.

"I tell you what, I'm going to sneak some popcorn up in here tomorrow because knowing Ms. B she may have some freaky deaky stuff on that tape," Tyree replied. "Our teacher is not a freak," Lesa said before telling Tyree to stop talking nonsense.

After Barker snapped out of her thoughts about what she overheard she began answering questions.

"What about the smoke? Are they ever going to get rid of it?" asked Sherrie. "I'm not sure, but I do know it's not fair. It's non-smoking throughout the buildings except on the gaming floor. State officials know smoking is bad for our health. So they terminated smoking in malls, at restaurants, in bars and other public places, yet it was okay for dealers to get secondhand smoke blown in our faces. We're human beings with families that love us, too, but that just goes to show you the love of money is the root of all evil. Of course, we always had the choice to resign, but rarely did anyone quit. Good question, Sherri. Next."

"Have any players ever tried to make you mad intentionally?" Troy hollered as if Barker was way across the room.

"Oh yes indeed. Players know exactly what dealers dislike and come to the table doing all kinds of unsanitary stuff," Barker said. "One time a player came to my table, spit in his hand and then tried to hand me his cash. I told him he'd better go wash his hands and I wanted to see the water still dripping from his hands before I touched his money. He never returned to my table. Some players chewed tobacco, spat in a plastic cup then had the nerve to sit the cup on the table like we wanted to look at a cup of saliva all day. It's grotesque. And women always came to the table with their breasts hanging out, like I really wanted to stare at them all day. There are just some body parts women need to keep to themselves. I'm telling you, you haven't seen anything until you experience a dealer's life in the casino." Barker took a second to apologize to Troy for going a little off topic and explained that when she started talking about her past her adrenaline started pumping.

"Do dealers receive bonuses? Lesa asked.

"Do dealers receive what? Bonuses! Puleeze. We were lucky if we even got a pat on the back" Barker said, sounding incredulous over the question. "Only upper management received bonuses, the people that were not around inhaling smoke all day. They could take days off anytime they wanted. Management should have been on the floor inhaling smoke and taking the insults, criticism and abuse that dealers experienced every day so they could see have seen how it felt. After one day experiencing what we go through I bet you they'd change the rules for sure. They got paid big salaries and took lavish vacations, and on top of that they made up rules as the days, weeks and months went by. Management was the worst when it came to knowing dealers' needs. They didn't care about us because if they did they would have given us bonuses for all the hard work we did and headaches we put up with daily – not to mention for working with people with so many attitudes including our supervisors. Lesa, I could go on all day about management, but like I said we have to cut the class short today. Next."

"What do you think players expect from dealers?" Helen inquired.

"Well, most players think dealers are their parents, doctors, psychologists, friends, lawyers, advisers and judges. You name it, and they think that's our role. Players always asked dealers what we thought and what we would do if it was our money. I used to think to myself the players should have gotten up and left. I used to hear players lie to their family all the time saying they were somewhere else, especially when they were talking to their children. How could you let money be more important than your family? All I could do was shake my head. Next question." Barker pointed at James.

"Do players know when to stop gambling?"

"No. They all said the same 'ole tired lines. 'This is my last hand. Or when I make X amount of money I'm leaving' It was very rare that they left with money because they continued playing until they were flat broke. What a way to let the devil rule you. You're next, Shane."

"Did you ever gamble?" she asked.

"Yes I did, and I regret it because I really thought since I was a dealer I had some type of luck. I finally realized I was acting just like the players. I hoped on striking it rich, but anybody who put his or her hopes in winning at the devil's palace needed prayer to be delivered. I found out the hard way there was no such thing as luck. You were either blessed or cursed. God blessed me to help me stop gambling. Amen."

"Ms. B, we're here for you and we're ready to watch the videotape with you," James said. "We want to help you move on with your life. You're a good teacher and we respect you dearly." Tears escaped from Barker's big brown eyes as the class gave her a group hug.

"Why thank you, James and class. I really appreciate the encouragement," Barker responded emotionally. "Okay class. It's about that time. Tomorrow I want to read letters from ex-students and dealers. And you should feel free to write me letters also about this class or how things are going with you once this class is over. It's always a pleasure to keep in contact with my former students."

Barker prayed prior to dismissing class. God, I thank you, and please give me the strength and courage to get through watching the videotape. And I thank you once more for blessing me with such a caring class. In Jesus' name I pray. Amen." The class said amen. As the students left the room they clapped and gave each other hi-fives, as if they'd just won the Super Bowl or hit the lottery.

A half an hour later Barker was a nervous wreck and in her office contemplating. *What am I'm going to do with myself? What if I don't like what I see on that tape?* She retrieved her messages. BEEP. Barker it's Tracey. I just want you to know you can get through this trying time, I'm here for you and you can call me anytime. God Bless you.

What was all that about, Barker wondered. *I guess I'll find out Friday huh?*

BEEP. Hey girl, Steve and I got back early so call me when you're free so we can pray together. Barker knew she didn't have much time so she decided to return her best friend's call when she got home. BEEP. Hi, Ms. B. This is Tundra. I just hope you make it through Friday. I heard from my parents that a lot was going on with you that you don't even know about. I'll see you in the morning and continue to pray for more strength.

Who are her parents? Do they even know me? Barker raised an eyebrow while pondering that last message. She felt she was ready to watch the videotape and tried convincing herself every chance she got. Barker scratched her head and her ponytail started to loosen. She knew it was time to go home, wash her hair and settle down for the rest of the evening. She pressed line one and screamed through the intercom.

"Yes, Ms. B?"

"Make sure Mr. Kenny gets all of the students' signatures and a copy of their IDs so I'll have their correct information on file."

"You got it!" Mona shouted back through the intercom.

Barker lost track of time while writing in her daily journal. The oversized Grandfather clock made a soft ding dong sound she didn't recognize because she was never there past 6 p.m.

She gathered her belongings then sashayed toward the elevators. As she reached ground level, she got lost in thought. *I know Friday is going to be hard for me. I just need to know what happened to me and who am I. Why are there so many secrets? How did I end up teaching this class? I want a family to enjoy. I have to go home and watch the same old soap operas replaying the same old scenes – sex, drama, drugs and death. Who's cheating on whom, etc. Hold up. This sounds just like the industry, a soap opera for real. God delivered me from that place and now he needs to deliver me from soap operas as well. No more TV for me. If I want my life to be right I have to get right.* Barker continued walking down the long hallway until she reached the front entrance. The large tan and black desk struck a pose parallel to the long glass-door entrance where the security guard was stationed.

Kenny hurriedly straightened up in his chair as he heard Barker coming down the hall toward him.

"Good night, Mr. Kenny," Barker said while thinking Kenny was trying to act as if he hadn't gotten busted for being asleep on the job.

"Good night, Ms. B."

Barker turned around to wave good night, just in time to see her receptionist. All of a sudden her sleepy eyes were wide open.

"Well, a good night to you both," she said, wondering whether Mona was embarrassed or ashamed.

Mona waved good night, as if she wasn't embarrassed or ashamed, and resumed giving Kenny pleasure. Barker knew Mona didn't know what she was getting herself into, but she

also knew Mona was grown and it was her life and her business. She decided to just leave it alone.

Barker started to pick out letters for class the next day. After
about an hour she dozed off on her gray plaid loveseat. The
telephone rang and the loud sound startled her half to death.
She jumped up and her letters flew all over the place. It looked
like over-sized confetti was pouring down in her living room.
Who's calling me this time of night?

"Hello," she growled.

"Janae, didn't I tell you to call me? It's a little after 11.
What's the problem?" Malaika snapped.

"No problem. I fell asleep. After I took a hot shower and
ate my dinner I began picking over the letters I'm going to
read to my class tomorrow. Please don't take it personally. I
was going to call." Barker lied because she didn't want to hurt
Malaika's feelings.

She grumbled while picking up the papers from her burgundy padded carpet with one hand and managing the phone
with her other one. She didn't realize how many of her past
students had written her over the years.

"Well never mind picking out those letters right now. Steve wants to pray with you," Malaika said. "Pick up the other
line Pooky."

Barker heard Steve say ok Pooky and wondered why they
called each other that silly name.

"God Bless, Janae," Steve said.

"Hey, Steve," Barker said in a sleepy voice. Steve got
straight to the point without hesitation.

"Jesus, I ask you to give Janae strength and peace of mind
as she watches the videotape on Friday. We all know this is

going to open and close some doors for her. Lord I am asking you to shut the doors of confusion, stress, blackouts and depression and opens a door of deliverance for Janae Barker. She is our sister in Christ and she needs our support as well as we need hers. God allow your angels to be in that room and rebuke any negative spirits from the videotape. I bond that right now, and in the name of Jesus I pray. Amen."

"Amen. Honey that was great," Malaika shouted as if she'd caught the Holy Ghost.

"Amen, Steve. You sure do know how to pray. I'm ready to dance and shout myself," Barker said sincerely. "Thank you all so much for loving and caring for me. Goodnight Steve. I'll talk to you tomorrow, Malaika."

"Good night. Love ya!" Malaika shouted once more in Barker's ear.

"I love you more," Barker whispered.

Barker rubbed her eyes. She was grateful for Malaika's and Steve's support; she just didn't understand why they waited so darn late to call her.

The dial tone was the sweetest sound Barker's ears had heard all day. *God forgive me for almost dozing off during Steve's prayer.* Barker couldn't wait to get a good night's sleep and get the week over with. She got up and went in her bedroom so she could sleep in her plush Euro top bed instead of on her much less comfortable plaid couch.

DREAMS CAN LAST A LIFETIME
~THURSDAY~

Thursday was another beautiful day for which Barker was thankful. She had gotten a good night's rest after having prayer with Malaika and Steve. She wasn't upset over their call because she knew they meant well. She just wished they hadn't called so late. Her thoughts quickly switched back to the videotape, and she began fantasizing about regaining power over her life once she watched it.

Barker was feeling wonderful because she knew her past was about to be revealed. No matter what was on the videotape, she had to let it go and put it behind her. She looked forward to the great future God had in store for her.

"Good morning, Ms. Barker" Mona said as Barker passed her desk.

"Good Morning, Mona. One more day before Showtime at the Apollo."

After shutting the door behind her, Barker reached for the letters she would read in class only to realize she'd left the entire stack of them at home on her marble dinette table. In her rush to get to work – after all, tomorrow was the big day so the sooner she got through today the sooner she could watch the videotape – she had inadvertently left them. Barker thought about the letters she'd read the night before at home. Despite her honesty in class, there were still some students who became dealers anyway. Unfortunately, she didn't convince everyone to stay away from the industry, but at least she gave them a heads up so they wouldn't walk into it blind like she did. People had to make up their own minds about what they wanted out of life. After many years Barker chose not to live that type of life anymore. She wanted her freedom and her weekends back, and that's what she got. Her teaching job was just a stepping stone. Eventually she wanted to travel and preach God's word, but until then she would teach her classes. Even though she felt like she made it through, there was still something holding her back. Since she was closer to closure she could now checkmate her next move. Tomorrow, hopefully, everything would be revealed to her.

"Do you have any letters?" Barker asked Mona through the intercom.

"I have 20 letters in my filing cabinet that were sent direct-ly to your in-house mailbox over the last few months," Mona said as she cleared her throat.

"Twenty. Nah, that's too many. I just want to read 15 so the students could hear responses from real casino dealers." Mona brought Barker the stack of letters, and she spent the next 30 minutes reading them.

Barker prayed and all of the children said amen, which was a first but what she imagined would happen eventually. She informed the students she had some informative letters to read, to which Sherrie replied: "I never heard of a teacher teaching class from her personal possessions. This is a first."

"I just want you all to hear some of their actual experiences in the industry," Barker explained. "I'll read them all then answer questions afterwards. Remember to write down any questions you have about a letter so we can discuss your questions afterward." Barker took her letters and made two piles on her desk. As she read the letters the class was so silent you could hear a pin drop.

Letter One

Hi, Ms. Barker
I just want to thank you for giving me insight to the casino industry. After I thought it over I became a police officer. My husband decided to still become a dealer, and he developed a big gambling habit which became a problem in our household. Now we're headed for a messy divorce. I know I'll end up with nothing only because he gambled away all of our savings.

He really thought he could sit there all day and night while our children were missing love from him. Both of our cars were repossessed and our house is in foreclosure. Thanks for convincing me not to work there. You really have to be strong-minded to be in that place. I just couldn't understand why he complained that players lose all their money and all their common sense, but he was in the same damned boat.
Love Monique

Letter Two

Hello, Ms. B
Teach, I just want to tell you I still became a dealer and I married someone's ex husband about six months after their divorce. I know I'm wrong for that, but I fell in love with him. We always worked together and we grew interested in one another.

I'm still dealing and some of the supervisors get on my nerves. I just ignore them and do my job. And the players are so rude. One player had the nerve to call me a black bitch. Don't you know my supervisor didn't say anything in my defense? I gave that old white man one of the dirtiest evil eyes you could imagine. And guess what? When I got back from break her ass was gone.
Love Raiketa.

Letter Three

Dear Ms. B
Why did I think I could bring the house down? I tried gambling after work several times at different casinos and lost all of my money and now live paycheck to paycheck wishing just one good time I could beat the house. It looked so easy when I was dealing, but it was easier to lose my money. By any chance could I borrow $500 before the 5th to pay my rent? I promise to pay you back. Oh yeah, one more thing...A player went postal on the Blackjack table because he wanted the supervisor to stop laughing. How crazy is that? He lost all of his money and then he wanted to be in control. I just laughed to myself. Players be bugging...Thanx, Shantella

Letter Four

Hey,
I took your class a couple of years ago. I'm a single parent, and I cannot spend quality time with my children the way I want. I never have weekends off and I can't afford to call out. And even if I did call out they have a system by which I can't call out unless I'm sick. I work from 3 p.m. to 11 p.m. and my children are in bed by the time I get home. Please feel free to email me at dealerspikupspirits@aim.com. Help. I am dying and need to find a way out while still being able to take care of my family. By the way, my former supervisor got caught stealing to satisfy his drug habit. How weird is that? Hmmm. I don't know what he was

thinking, but then, I guess it's a pretty common place for junkies to steal to support their habits, and he was working in a casino around a ton of money. Oh well...

Love, your ex- student, Sandra D.

Letter Five

Hi, B.

I was determined to work in the casino business, and I was ready for any of those spirits to try to jump on me because I considered myself a real man. Well, this real man got in debt to the tune of $20,000 thanks to the industry and poor choices. I'm out of debt now and going back to school to become a businessman. I'm tired of looking at sick people.

What I mean by that is my co-workers complain and whine the whole eight hours. They already know what they're getting into once they step through the casino doors, so they should either roll with it or roll out. That's the way I feel. Sometimes I just wanted to say shut the hell up. Then of course players were mad they lost all of their money. This is just a sick place to work. But when you don't believe in yourself it's easy to get stuck right here in this industry. I'm better than that, and I'm going to prove it to me.

Thanks for the advice teacher.

Love, Eric

Letter Six

How are you doing? Teach.

I'm writing you to let you know I accepted Jesus Christ in my life and I cannot stand working in this casino anymore. The dealers get treated like yesterday's trash. We get no recognition from anyone. I have been working for over a year now, and not once have upper management come to meet me. Instead, I have to endure all types of profanity and loud music, watch couples who are in obviously unhealthy relationships and listen to complainers.

There are also players who lie to their families continuously just so they can gamble on my table all day. It's just the devil's palace up in here, and I'm asking The Lord to show me a way out. I know there's another way to make good, positive money.

P.S. You know before I got saved I had to curse a few players out. One time this guy was putting nasal spray up his nose at the table. And you know we're like a foot away from each other on the Blackjack table. I told him if just a smudge of snot touched me it was on. And another time a lady player threatened to throw her drink on me after accusing me of looking at her 70-year-old husband. Oh, I wanted any of them to get crunk and it would have been on. Other than that I'm good…
Carla

Letter Seven

Long time no hear from, Ms. Barker
I miss our talks we used to have over the phone. I know you have been wondering where I've been. Well, I'm in jail. Working around all of that money got real tempting, and I tried to steal $500 dollars a week. I was doing good until I got greedy. Well, you know the rest. The cameras caught me, and now I'm doing a year in this hell hole.
Write me back, Kenya Dee
Ps. Address; 126-Correctional Facility
J-lid Drive, Wawa, N.J.

Letter Eight

What's cooking, teach?
Let me first tell you that I didn't listen to you. After being in the casino so many years I've been promoted and demoted and now

two other chicks that have been in this business for only six months are supervising me. Isn't that a slap in the face?

Teach, my God-sister has been on the job for 14 years and they laid her off and told her to re-apply for a part-time position. I'm telling you this house is grimy. When we start making a little money, accruing vacation time and benefits they're ready to fire us. It's not fair at all. I'm so ready to fight upper management. One Love, Adam

Letter Nine

My aunt died of lung cancer and she never smoked a day in her life. It's not fair that every other area is no-smoking but the dealers have to inhale all that second-hand smoke. What about out health and our families? Does anyone care about us? Now my aunt is gone. What do I tell her children? They are only 2 and 3 years old, respectively.

You always told us if we had anything on our mind to tell you. Teach...You were so right. If I had nothing but middle fingers on my hands I would put both hands up to the industry.

Sorry teach. I know it sounds harsh, but that's how I feel. Forgive me for speaking this way but I'm hurting. Some justice has to occur. THEY SHOULD BAN SMOKING ON THE CASINO FLOOR. By the way, the players will stop smoking to gamble, but why should we have to gamble our lives with smoke?
Korun.

Letter Ten

Hey, Ms. B
I did exactly what you said and went back to school. Wow! I'm a nurse. But do you remember Kysha? She's working and slaving for that industry. She never gets weekends or holidays off. We can't even hang out without her snapping on someone. Her whole

attitude has changed. But as for me, I'm happy and stress free. Thanks for your class ☺
Ayanna

Letter Eleven

Yo, B
Let me tell how I got into it with the pit boss today. They make up all these rules and we go by them. But if a player gets mad or has a lot of money they change the rules as if we're not doing our jobs. Granted, we dealers make mistakes, but we're under a lot of pressure and we need to know our own team members and co-workers have our backs. I saw that my own supervisor didn't have my back. I got in trouble for doing the right thing. I underpaid a player and I caught it on my own. We found the player; paid him his correct dough and I still got written up...
Smoke

Letter Twelve

Wazzup, Teach?
How have you been, Ms. Barker? I'm dealing and handling it. Just one issue I have is with my co-dealers. I get so sick and tired of them complaining about late breaks. Dealer this and dealer that are always late for their breaks, but when those dealers come back they smile in their face like they never said a word about them. They need to confront the person and tell them how they feel and stop with all that jibber jabber. Nobody wants to hear that bull for eight hours.
Mike

Letter Thirteen

Everything you taught us was so true. I like dealing because it's fun meeting different people. I guess you have to have a great

sense of humor to work in a place like this. The only problem I have is they always mess up my paycheck and I have to wait for the next week to get paid. They need to start cutting my check out right at the cashier booth. I have more than enough bills to pay, and I need to get my money on time like everybody else working in this joint. Anyway, I hope your classes are coming along fine.
Iris

Letter Fourteen

Mrs. B,
I just read in the newspaper they're building more of those devil worshiping palaces. It's a shame people can't even help the homeless but they can build more casinos. I gambled my whole life's savings away and now I live in the mission. Anyway, I was tired of working there because there was too much favoritism for me. Some people got in trouble and others didn't and they both made the same 'ole mistakes. Like the saying goes, it's not what you know but who you know.
Love, Aniyah

Letter Fifteen

Ms B,
How are you? Fine I hope. I think my whole class became dealers after we spent the week with you. Now all we do is complain about how we should have listened. Man, this place is crazy. I can't stand making under minimum wage. And that smoke drives me crazy. But I need the money so I just dummy up and deal while my insides scream for help. If every dealer chipped in $10 a week we could rent a billboard to inform the players we work for tips. I believe our checks would look a whole a lot healthier if we did that.
Peace, Shakiya.

DREAMS CAN BECOME YOUR REALITY
~FRIDAY~

B arker felt somewhat traumatized after reading the letters. But even still she thanked God and sang TGIF, TGIF, TGIF. She couldn't care less about being out of tune. Her spirit was on the right key with The Lord, and that's all that mattered.

Lord, God Jesus I ask you to clothe me in your spirit right now, Barker thought. *Drown me in your blood and give me the strength to watch the videotape.*

Barker stood to wipe off her knees and continued getting dressed. She put her jet black curly hair in a bun before slipping into a white, green, yellow and orange strapless spring dress with matching white open-toe shoes. Barker felt as good as she looked, even though her subconscious was telling her not to watch the videotape.

Meanwhile, back at the *REBUILD YOURSELF CENTER* Tony was preparing for Barker's moment of truth. He had to set up early because he wanted to have the entire routine done to his perfection. Tony had placed Dr. Keith, Evonne and Ms. Tracey in the room next door to where Barker would show the videotape. They were all prepared for the worst but hoping for the best.

Evonne and Keith went over all the procedures just in case Barker went into distress or fainted. Dr. Keith had spoken very highly of Ms. Barker and believed she could defeat the videotape this time around. He believed she could watch it in its entirety and get through it. Dr. Keith straightened his glasses while remarking about how much healthier and stronger Barker appeared this time around. Evonne nodded in agreement. "Yes, she does look much better than the last time she tried to attempt to watch the videotape." Ms. Tracey, Evonne and Dr. Keith all waved at Tony to assure him they had everything under control.

Tony wanted to ensure they all were on the same page. "I hope you'll all carefully observe Barker's reactions. From this room you can watch her on this TV and it will give you a heads-up on her moves. I don't want Barker to see any of you here today because she'll think I don't trust her. I do trust her, but I'm taking extra precautions in case things don't go as she planned for them to go." Tony closed the door behind him.

Barker informed Mona to take messages for her and not to interrupt her class under any circumstances. She also instructed Mona to ensure her students were comfortable before she entered the room. Mona walked about three steps ahead of Barker and could see the class preparing to watch the videotape. She could also see Charlie's Angels – Dr. Keith, Tracey and Evonne – next door.

Barker strolled down the hall as if she owned the building. She felt good inside and out. *Once the children lay eyes on me they'll think I got a complete makeover,* she thought. Barker gave most full-figured women a run for their money back in the day when she was in high school. No doubt she was among the sexiest girls in her class and had it going on. Even today she still had it. And she knew it.

Barker walked in the class and got straight to business by praying. Then she explained what an early push was. "If you do the first hour you get to go home a half hour early," she told her students. "But that was only if the dealers agreed because it was not mandatory but instead a courtesy. Then we had what you call an early out, or E.O. sheet. If the industry had extra dealers you would be the next one off the list to go home – if you signed it. All employee schedules were done weekly, including the tables dealers were assigned to work. And when it came to schedules, who you knew could take you a long way. Placers were people who could deal or supervise, and they were invaluable and used a lot by the industry.

Besides the supervisors were several bosses that ran the area. It appeared they just walked back and forth and didn't do much. There were some good area bosses, but for the most part they had their favorites, too. Finally there was a house manager who overlooked the area bosses – placers and dealers. It was like a chain reaction, and dealers got the heat from them all – including the players."

Barker froze as she glanced at the television.

"Get off of me. Why are you putting this white jacket on me? Who the hell are you? So now my life is over? This industry had no compassion for me or my family. All they wanted me to do was come to work and make them money. They wanted me to slave by dealing to customers eight hours a day even on holidays and other days that were special days to me. What about me, Mr. Casino? When all you

big shots were raking in bonuses, going on fancy trips and getting people to fill in for you when you needed to take off, it was all good. You forgot about the people suffering who actually brought in all the money for you, huh? Yea, I and about 800 other dealers were the ones who had to take the abuse from the customers. We were the front-line servers for the industry. We were also the first ones to be fired. Yea I'm pissed off, Mr. Casino. You started me off at $4.00 an hour when minimum wage was $7.50. How did the state let you pull that off? Then you wanted us to work for tips yet we couldn't even mention tips and we had to drop whatever tips came our way in the tote box, Mr. Casino.

What about bonuses for us dealers? Last year someone in upper management, not even 'The Man', received a $1.1 million bonus. For what, I ask you? I never saw him, let alone heard anything about him. I guess he did the industry right somehow to earn a bonus like that. Why couldn't I get a free massage at least once a month? Bending over these tables sure did hurt my back and feet. Then I had to work under those terrible conditions and endure trash talk from players just because they had money.

So you thought that was fair? After all, I was a human being also. Oh and why was it that the casino floor was the only location in the casino that still allowed smoking? Didn't we need to breathe, too? Yes, we did. So your thinking killed us dealers, huh? It's not fair that we had to inhale all that second-hand smoke just to bring a couple of dollars to the industry. You really didn't care about us. And I had no job security in that place because after so many years you just kicked folks out the door. I was hip to your games, though. You wanted all part-timers so you wouldn't have to give us benefits or vacation time. Mr. Casino, you were just so greedy for money.

You didn't even give us decent food to eat or appliances with which to heat our food in the break room. I wondered what you do with all your money. Did you ever come down on the floor? Better yet, did you ever try to work a shift? I guarantee you wouldn't have lasted a shift. The supervisors you had working for you complained about their breaks all day. Why couldn't you give them set breaks? They sounded like a bunch of kindergarteners in my ear. "Oh, she took five extra minutes." "Oh, she's one minute late." Just get over it. You took the position so deal with it. But as for me, I was tired of working for you, giving you every weekend, every special day – my life. Every day off request I put in got denied. Why did you even give out request forms? Then most dealers thought they deserved more than other dealers, but I didn't know why because we all went through the same situation. You gave us sick time, but when we called out sick we got penalized. So did you really give us sick time? Answer me, Mr. Casino? I dare you to fake like you did something for us dealers. You took everything away from us. The only real money we had to depend on was our retirement and now you've taken that. Yes, I was unhappy everyday for years and years. I watched and listened as people threatened to quit or wished to get fired from this sick place. I had never seen people so discontented until I began working in this industry. When they got fired they jumped up and down shouting for joy as if they were just released from prison.

I was tired of slaving for your company while customers with foul, liquored-up breath burped in my face. And let's not talk about their attitudes. All you told me was to smile because the customers were always right. Well, Mr. Casino, I'm here to tell you they were not always right. They were nothing but cheaters and liars. They were greedy, rude and nasty and it was just plain sickening the way they craved the money. They thought they were going to win, but we took all the heat when they started complaining because nine times out of 10 the only ones that complained were those that lost, and they got mad at us like we had done something to them.

Why give us dealers a hard time? Yea, I know some dealers deserve to be corrected. There was so much going on, but you managers should have revised things instead of always trying to write us up for dumb, immature stuff. I remember just as plain as yesterday a time when your area boss called me an inmate and told me he was the warden while pointing his fingers in my face. If he had been just a tad closer I probably would have smacked the taste out of his mouth. He did the right thing by fixing his glasses and moving on. Mr. Casino, did you know that? I bet you didn't. Oh, I forgot your area bosses were always right, too. So, as you can see, we dealers had it bad. We were stuck in the middle and we were always wrong. No

*matter what we did or said we should have done things differently
according to the industry rules. By the way, speaking of rules…They
changed whenever you felt like changing them. You printed out a
memo and there you had it. You had changed the rules. I wondered
whether that was legal? I worked a whole 40- hour week and then
you messed up my check and I had to wait two more weeks for you to
fix it. What about me and my bills? Was it fair that you got all this
money and you couldn't even cut me a check on the spot? Mr.
Casino I was so ready to fight you.*

*I blame you for my husband's death and the deaths of my three
little ones. How could you deny me a day off to spend with my
family? We were going to stay home and play family games, but
because you denied me the day off my husband took the children up
the road to visit his mother. Along the way the car slid on some ice
and crashed into a telephone pole, causing the electric wires to
disconnect and swing into the car. Mr. Casino I dare you! You have
denied me for the last time."*

"Somebody help! She's about to jump," someone yelled
frantically. Barker moved swiftly toward the open window on
the eighth floor. She reached for the wooden latch and before
the class knew it, Barker's three-inch heel got stuck in the
crack of the ledge. Barker shouted help… help… help… but
unfortunately it was too late. Ebony let out a powerful
NOOOOOOOOOOOOOOO!

Chapter 2

TAMAL

I t all began when Tamal witnessed a terrible incident in the Jackson household. After that dreadful night he made a vow to move out of Camden County for once and for all.

"Baby are you ready?" Tamal asked cautiously. He had really thought long and hard about whether to let his future baby's mother go with him to Philadelphia to begin a new life. Tamal knew deep down it was the right thing to do because two parents were better than one. This he knew without question. Also, there were enough African-American children living in single-parent homes as it was. But then, his father was in his household which wasn't always necessarily a good thing...

"Yea, as soon as I spend a little Deptford Mall time with Sasha," Fancy whispered to Tamal. As she patted down her weave, Fancy thought about how she couldn't wait to get over the bridge to Philly so she and Tamal could spend every day and every night together. Sneaking behind Sasha's back had gotten to be too much this past year. The only person she could trust with her secrets was her Aunt Brenda.

"Tamal, it's finally happening," Fancy said. "We're going to be together as one after all." Fancy sounded ecstatic as she spoke, but Tamal ignored her comment.

"Corvette and I will pick you up from Deptford Mall so hurry up and finish packing," Tamal said. He told fancy to text him after she finished spending time with her cousin, Sasha. As soon as she hung up her Blackberry Sasha beeped the horn for her. Sasha had taken her new old whip for a spin up and down Haddon Street in Camden. Her mother Brenda had saved a couple of dollars to buy her a used 2002 silver Camry for graduation. Brenda was a proud mother and would have done anything to keep Sasha safe and happy.

Corvette Ford was a legal secretary for Frisby & Trappe, a big law firm in Center City. She had been working part time on ways to get contributions for families in need. Her body reminded you of Alicia Keys, but her tush was 15 pounds heavier than Keys'. When she was a little girl the boys called her brick house. Now the men called her Amazon.

"Here's your very own apartment," Corvette said while walking the happy couple to their townhouse on Philly's south side. Thanks to donation from wealthy citizens Corvette was able to pay their rent for the first three months.

"Ah man, thanks," Tamal said to Corvette. While hugging her, his finger accidently got caught in her spaghetti straps dress, prompting him to say, "My bad."

"No issue here, Tamal" Corvette said. She liked a man's touch, but Tamal was far from her type because he wasn't married. Corvette gave Tamal and Fancy a map showing nearby grocery stores, banks, restaurants and daycare centers. Besides finding them a place to live she secured jobs for each of them: Fancy as an assistant secretary and Tamal as a casino dealer.

"Now remember Tamal, you have to be at Legacy at 7:30 p.m. sharp Friday night," Corvette said. "My mother will be waiting for you. Her name is Ms. Ford."

"Wow, what a name. Corvette Ford," Tamal said with admiration. "I'm scared to ask you what your middle name is."

"It's Shevy with an S," Corvette said as she winked at him.

"Ok people. That's enough flirting, Tamal I know she looks as good as her names sounds, but you do have your baby's mother in the room here. Besides, I think Ms. Corvette Shevy Ford has better things to do than to hang out with us two love birds," Fancy said with a jealous tone in her voice. Tamal looked at both women and thought he should had left Fancy's ass back in Camden. But he didn't so now he had to say goodbye to flirting.

"Corvette, before you leave can I ask you why you're doing this for us?" Fancy tried not to sound ungrateful but couldn't help thinking it was pretty ironic that Corvette met them as they exited The Camden Women's Center a month ago and now thanks to her they owned a townhome in Philadelphia. "Like I said before Fancy, it's just business," Corvette replied. She knew she needed to prove to The Capital that she could help a least three families each quarter to consistently receive grants. It was like Section 8, but different. For most of Corvette's life she felt in her heart she wanted to help families in need. Corvette had been working on family home assistance for more than three years now. If she could prove she could help one family get off the streets and assist them in finding promising jobs the governor would donate more money to her homeless fund. Even though she was a legal secretary she didn't see herself going far with Frisby & Trappe because she let down her guard and fell in love with another woman's husband. "Fancy, just look at it this way. This project is my Plan B," Corvette said. "Just consider it a blessing in disguise." She closed their screen door behind her and left.

Chapter 3

SASHA

Sasha Rusty always had to be the center of attention. She was one of the most real girls that grew up in Camden County. If you didn't know about Sasha Rusty, shame on you. Everyone in high school used to tease her and her cousin Fancy by flipping their last name and saying "here comes Rusty Sasha and Rusty Fancy."

Sasha often asked her mother why she didn't have her father's last name, but Brenda would quickly tell her to get over the name calling because when she was in school they called her Rusty, too.

Sasha's father was an alcoholic, and her mother never fooled with him after she was born. At least that was Brenda's story and she stuck to it – until the day Sasha found out the truth.

Everyone respected Sasha Rusty around the hood after she smashed footprints in Sarah Cook's face. Sarah was considered the toughest chick at Camden high, but one fateful day she teased Fancy for the last time. Sasha took Sarah by her long ponytail, twisted it around her hand, slammed her head on the hallway floor – BAM-BAM-BAM – as if she just busted the best wrestling move of all time. Eventually Sarah was saved by the bell. Sasha was suspended for 10 days, but once she returned to school not only had she earned respect but Fancy got respect as well.

No matter what was bothering her, Sasha Rusty never walked around with a bad taste in her mouth. She had the heart, balls and guts to spit it out without hesitation. Sometime she knew she was wrong, but she stuck by her guns no matter what.

Sasha had deep secrets of her own and others that she didn't bother sharing with her friends. Fancy Rusty was her first cousin on her mother's side and the two got very close during high school. Fancy's mother Mary got very ill from brain cancer, and Brenda was the only sister willing to take Fancy in.

"Stop crying, Fancy. It will be all right," Sasha said softly while wiping Fancy's tears from her eyes. "I know, but I know I'll miss my mom. She was everything to me. Now look at me." Sasha looked closely as her cousin kept talking and noticed how helpless she looked. "I'm only 16. She's not going to see me go to my prom, graduate or get married. And Sasha, what about when I have children?" Sasha took Fancy by the hand and guided her to the back exit of the church for some from fresh air.

"Your mother is resting now and eventually you'll be just fine. We're here for you. Hey, I'm your sister/cousin because as long as I'm living I've got your back." Sasha gave Fancy a reassuring hug.

"Thanks, cousin for being here for me," Fancy said. The girls hugged again as they walked toward Brenda, who waited on them at the car. During their last two years of high school Sasha had to fight for Fancy. Fancy was the new pretty girl at school and to all the boys she looked like a tender piece of steak while the other girls reminded them of their mothers' leftover chicken.

Sasha tried warning Fancy not to get involved with Tashad Trader. It was Tashad's last year of high school and all the ladies fell in love with him as if they were hypnotized by his bright green eyes. When Tashad laid eyes on Fancy he gave up all the other girls, including Janelle, his high school sweetheart. Cheerleader, musician, singer or team captain – titles meant zilch. Tashad was no longer looking for the best person in the group because he was vulnerable to Fancy.

"Excuse me good looking!" Tashad said politely while brushing up against Fancy's backside.

"Oh, you're excused Twinkle," Fancy flirted.

"Oh, what honor do I have to be called Twinkle?" Tashad asked.

"Every time I see you I get a twinkle in my pants because your eyes put a fire in my soul." Fancy had a bad sense of humor, but it seemed to work for Tashad. And the rest, as they say, was history. Fancy and Tashad were an item until her last couple of months in high school. Once Sasha found out Tashad had gotten Janelle pregnant, she had to figure out how to tell her sister/cousin who was in serious denial when it came to Tashad.

"Fancy, what's up?" Sasha peeked into their room.

"Nothing much, Sasha. I'm just getting ready for our prom."

Sasha felt awful at that very moment. *How am I going to break the news that Janelle is about to have Tashad's baby?* Sasha being Sasha she knew she had to tell her sooner rather than later.

"Fancy, Janelle is pregnant." Sasha spit it out just like that.

"Wow. That's good. Now maybe she'll leave me and my man alone," Fancy said, not knowing Tashad was the father. She started rambling about how Janelle kept calling him.

"You know she called Tashad three times last night while we were enjoying 'Jumping the Broom.' I was trying to have some 'us' time since this is my last year of high school and his first year of college. As it is we barely get to spend time with each other now." Sasha looked at Fancy with an incredulous expression. *Wow! She's blinder than I thought.*

"Cousin, you know me right," Sasha began. "And much as I had your back with all of those jealous hateful chicks who didn't like you because you were Tashad Trader's girl you know I'd never say anything if I didn't do my homework first. What I speak is the truth. You know that, right?"

"Yes," Fancy replied, wondering where this was going.

"So, do you ever wonder why Janelle kept calling Tashad?"

"Yea, I know her heart was broken and she never got over Tashad," Fancy said. "He let me listen to the message she left him, like when we first started dating." Sasha rubbed the top of Fancy's weave.

"Cousin, cousin, cousin. There's no easy way to say this. Tashad is the father of Janelle's soon to-be-baby," Sasha said as Fancy slapped her hand off her hair.

"How long have you known this?" Fancy said, rolling her eyes. "Oh please speak now or does the cat have your tongue all of a sudden?" Sasha had never seen Fancy so upset, but she knew she could whip her like cake mix if it came to it. Sasha chose to be calm during this emotional time for Fancy. *Oh no baby, Tashad has your brain,* Sasha wanted to say. She knew after all Fancy had been through with losing her mother, she didn't deserve *this* crap.

"I just found out this morning. Tamal saw Janelle on her way to the doctor and learned she's six months pregnant. She gave Tamal the entire scoop."

"Now it all makes sense why she kept blowing up his phone and when I asked about it all he says was she's bugging," Fancy said. "Well, I'm not doing anything else with his ass." Fancy ran out of the room hysterical and went to the prom with Tamal instead.

Graduation day came and then all Fancy wanted to do was get as far away from Camden as she possibly could. Her mother had left her a small pension, and Fancy was able to collect it now because she was of age. She gave her Aunt Brenda a thank-you card and $2,000 before taking Sasha shopping at Deptford Mall to say her final goodbye.

They were eating and reminiscing about the good 'ole times when suddenly a teardrop fell from Fancy's eyes.

"What's wrong, Fancy? Tashad is not still bothering you is he?" Sasha asked with whipping his ass on her mind.

"No he's not. After Janelle had their baby boy he told me once he looked in his eyes he fell instantly in love with him. I spoke to him two more times after that." At that moment Sasha wanted to kick Janelle's and Tashad's asses for having her cousin feeling so much pain and for their deception. But she remembered the way Fancy got him and thought *what goes around comes around.*

"Sasha, once we walk out this mall you'll be heading back home to Camden while I'll be heading over the bridge to Pennsylvania," Fancy said in a timid, low voice.

"Huh what, what do you mean?" Sasha felt lost and confused but didn't want to show Fancy her soft side so she just went with the flow.

"Cousin, you know I believe in following your dreams so wherever you are just give me a phone call from time to time so I'll know you're safe." Sasha and Fancy embraced for five long minutes before wiping tears from their eyes.

"I'm going to miss you cousin."

"Me, too. What about my mom?"

"Oh, Aunt Brenda knows exactly how I feel and what's going on because I wrote it in the card I gave her," Fancy said. As they walked out the mall entrance they saw a red Corvette with a license plate that read "It's me." The car was waiting for Fancy.

"You sure you'll be all right?" Sasha questioned, worried about her cousin.

"Yea," Fancy said with confidence. "I'm sure Sasha. I love you and I'll see you soon."

Fancy eventually lived up to her word, although she didn't speak to Sasha until many years later.

Chapter 4

BREAK-ROOM

"Hey, how are you today?" Braze asked while embracing Leona as they entered the break room.

"I'm doing just fine, allowing God to take care of all my problems" Leona replied while continuing to speak as she flipped the pages in her King James Bible.

"You know Braze, God says in Philippians 4:19 He will supply all your needs according to His riches in glory in Christ Jesus," Leona said as if she was preaching.

"I hear ya," J.T. said, imitating a Holy Ghost shout.

"J.T., you know you can't say anything to Leona without her giving you a Jesus speech," Braze said while she and J.T. clapped like they had just won the World Series. In the meantime Leona walked away putting her Bible back in her locker. *God please excuse them for they do not know what they're saying,* she thought.

"Who's the new dealer J.T.?" Braze inquired.

"Oh right there," J.T. said while pointing. "That's Tamal Jackson, and he's a cool dude. He and his baby's mother just moved here from Camden. Corvette, Ms. Ford's daughter, got him a job here and got his baby's mother, Fancy, a job working for Leona's husband's law firm Frisby and Trappe." J.T. ran Tamal's information down like he was an FBI agent.

"Oh yea, my husband told me Corvette had a new best friend at the firm. Every time a new assistant comes in the building Corvette makes good friends with her until she starts playing home wrecker," Leona said.

"How come she never tried that with you, Leona?" Braze asked. "Jesus has us covered. And I dare a woman to come against the blood of Jesus," Leona quickly replied. "My husband Lamont might not be walking in His light, but I pray for him every morning before he leaves for work." Then Leona glanced at the clock hanging directly in front of her on the otherwise naked wall.

"Put it like this. I leave it to Jesus to handle my problems, unlike you Braze," Leona said obviously bothered by the question. "What's that supposed to mean?" Leona. "I know I'm living in sin and haven't married my children's father yet. Perhaps I'm waiting for him to get a better job."

Meanwhile, J.T. sat quietly in the back getting better acquainted with Tamal.

"What do you know? Our 20 minutes are up, and we have to get back on the floor," J.T. said. "Come on ladies. You can start on round two during the next break." The dealers quickly returned to the gaming floor.

Braze knew she was wrong for not marrying her high-school sweetheart Jott Stagger. In Jott's younger days he was a fabulous guitar player and affectionately called his guitar Karma. He played in a jazz band, Jott and the Grand Crew, for many of years until the day the man with the red Mohawk told him he was discontinuing the jazz act because one of the band members was charged with rape. "Your band will have a bad reputation because of the rape charge, no matter how good you guys are," he said while putting his pen back in his shirt pocket. Jott felt defeated once again. He had planned to beg Braze to marry him, but he knew she would never marry him now given his gig was over. Mohawk man gave Jott two week's severance pay and told him he hoped everything worked out with him and his future wife. Croy, one of the

Grand Crew members, said Braze wasn't going to marry him in the first place. Now Jott had to face the music that Croy was right. Jott gave her two beautiful children, Brody and Cindy, and she was his first and only sweetheart, she thought. They had been together since high school.

Braze felt in her heart Leona was right and she shouldn't be living in sin. She continued daydreaming about Jott, who cared for her dearly, knowing if he ever found out the truth about her he'd die from a broken heart.

Chapter 5

BRAZE

"Hello honey. How was your night?" Jott asked. He was eager to lean forward to kiss the love of his life.

"Hey babes," Braze said while moving purposefully around the room to avoid his advances. Jott reached toward his fiancée, gesturing for a welcome-home kiss. Sadly, he realized she had her poker face on again, just as she nodded no.

"Baby I'm so tired tonight, and all I want to do is take a hot shower and get some sleep," Braze lied.

"Braze, I'm your fiancé and you don't satisfy my needs anymore. We haven't made love in three weeks. I'm fed up, Braze. Every time you come from work you're so tired," Jott said heatedly. Braze knew Jott was right. She was tired of making excuses about not wanting to have sex with him anymore. Being a dealer and taking on all of that stress for eight hours a day, five days a week for the last eight years had taken its toll on her. She wanted to tell Jott he had no idea what she was into and how she felt once she got home.

"Honey, on my day off I'll make love to you," Braze said. Jott didn't believe a word coming from Braze's mouth because she always used that same 'ole dry line. Her two days off flew by and she returned to work. She spent all of her time with the children on her off days. Then she told Jott she needed to get some rest before going back to work. Jott had had enough of Braze and her charades and didn't know how much longer he could take being neglected.

"You always use the children as an excuse, but they're old enough now to understand we need our special time, too," Jott pleaded. "I need you too, Braze. You give that company all of your attention and then the children get to spend time with you on your days off. What do I get? I get leftovers and crumbs, a peck on the cheek here and a cold shoulder there but no sex. Jott sat up in bed waiting for her response, but Braze had stopped listening to Jott long before he realized.

"Baby, it's almost 6 a.m. and I had a long night," Braze said. "And please lower your voice before the children hear us." Braze took off her work clothes and threw them on the floor with the rest of her dirty clothes. Then she hopped in the bed half naked wearing a bra and panties. The mattress sank further down on her side, and Jott's imagination started running wild. He leaned over, sucked on her earlobe and whispered, "What do you think about calling out tomorrow so we can spend some quality time together?" Braze looked at Jott like she'd never seen him before. "Braze, baby, what's wrong? Why are you staring at me like I'm an intruder?" Braze got up from the bed and walked out the room as if Jott was never there. "Fine, sleep on the couch again. It doesn't matter to me Braze."

The truth was Jott felt like Braze had taken a steak knife and cut deep into his heart until the blood was drained. He wanted his love back and he was tired of playing Mr. Perfect stay-at-home daddy. After Jott lost his job, instead of pursuing his dream of being a famous jazz musician he decided to be stay-at-home daddy-dearest for the children's sake. B.B King lyrics played repeatedly in Jott's mind.

The thrill is gone
The thrill is gone away
The thrill is gone Baby

The thrill is gone away
You know you done me wrong baby
And you'll be sorry one day.

Braze kept tossing and turning on the couch as she stared at the ceiling. She knew she was wrong for not giving Jott the loving he deserved. Jott was a wonderful man and father. Braze knew in her heart she didn't crave Jott the way he desired her. She tried to think of ways to tell him they needed to go their separate ways without hurting him. The children were 12 and 15 now, old enough to understand. But on the other hand she didn't want to hurt her children, so if she had to continue living a lie until they both reached 18 she would.

What type of mother would I be if I told the children I wanted to leave their father to be with my boss? How would Brody and Cindy take it? They would probably hate me forever. Braze knew how to pretend to be happy. If she had to continue rolling over every now and then so Jott could handle his business, she would. She would do anything to protect the hearts of her little ones. Braze really had a lot on her plate and sometimes wondered if she could devour it all.

She reminisced about her children and how she loved them so much. Then a bad thought crossed her mind. She frowned while laying her head on the pillow. *Braze, I told you to stop sleeping with that damned white boy. I will disown you if you ever have kids by him. You hear me, Braze?* Now she wondered whether she should have listened to her mother – not because of his race but because she found a new kind of love, or so she thought. Well, it was very much too late now because Braze has fallen out of love with Jott.

Chapter 6

TAMAL

"That's it, Tamal. "I can't take it anymore," Fancy yelled as loudly as she could. "You keep coming in this house early in the morning smelling like Ned the Wine-O." Fancy didn't realize Baby Tamal had awakened and was crying. Even though Tamal Jr. was 3-years-old he was still called Baby Tamal.

"Man, go to hell. I don't need you or my son," Tamal said. Once again he was drunk out of his mind and not understanding the damage he was doing to his family. Since Tamal began dealing Fancy had watched him drink his life away. *If I didn't know any better I'd swear he was his father all over again.*

Everybody knew Mr. Jackson was the drunk on their block. Fancy used to eavesdrop on Tamal's and Sasha's conversations and overheard the hurtful news one evening. She believed that was why she gave into Tamal, because she felt sorry for him. Fancy also felt in her heart Tamal didn't deserve her or her son. When a woman gets fed up there's nothing that can make her change her mind. Fancy dipped into her savings and thanked God for her stash. She moved to Chester, a suburban of Philadelphia. She had a plan and while Tamal was out bar hopping after work she decided to leave him for good. She and Corvette had become very close after working a couple of years together at Frisby and Trappe. Fancy had called Corvette crying her heart out a time or two and with everything that had gone on the last couple of years Corvette knew Fancy would be ready to vacate sooner or later.

"Honey, don't you worry about it," Corvette reassured her. "Since the condo is in Tamal's name only I can put you on the program as a single parent. We have two houses available right now as we speak."

"Thanks so much, Corvette. I don't know what has jumped into Tamal. It's like an evil spirit or something has possessed him." Fancy wanted to vacate the premises ASAP. She simply couldn't allow her son to live in danger anymore.

The ladies hung up, and sure enough Corvette's word was as good as gold. A week later Fancy moved into a beautiful townhome in Chester. Hopefully after getting a true glimpse of how their lives were supposed to manifest and realizing God wanted more for them, women as a whole would stop taking so much bullshit from men.

It had been several months and still no sign of Fancy or his son. Tamal really missed having them around the house. He knew he had a drinking problem and hoped one day he would get clean and get his family back. After a few shots of vodka Tamal's thoughts turned hateful and he childishly and spitefully removed all of Fancy's and Baby Tamal's pictures – even the ones in his wallet. He packed them away in a cardboard box and staggered across the street with them mumbling, *since the bitch took off with my son there's no need for me to keep their pictures in my crib.*

"So, do you know what you're doing?" Mrs. Greenwire asked Tamal. She could tell he was drunk and not in a proper state of mind. Tamal wobbled, confirming Mrs. Greenwire's suspicion. She weighed every bit of 220 pounds and was wearing her favorite light blue dress with her apron tied at the back of her neck.

"Yes, Mrs. Green. I'm getting rid of my Fancy and my son once and for good," Tamal staggered. *It's Greenwire, talking about getting rid of your Fancy and your son once and for good. Shit. You'd be lucky if they ever came back.* Mrs. Greenwire shook her head at Tamal, but nonetheless escorted him to her kitchen where she gave him a bowl of chicken broth soup and a glass of orange juice. It was the same meal she always gave her ex-husband after one of his drunken stupors. "Drink this, boy, and then sip on this broth," she said. "I'm not going to let you walk back across that street until I know you've sobered up. I don't know what's wrong with all of you children today. Every time there's an issue all you youngins try to drink or smoke your problems away. And then when you sober up from these poison products the same problems are still here."

Mrs. Greenwire turned around to see Tamal stretched out across her long Cherry wood table as if it was a king-sized bed, and she left him be until sunrise.

Mrs. Greenwire was like the grandmother everyone loved to have. She retired from teaching more than 15 years ago and was considered the neighborhood mother. She'd broken up a lot of fights, and nobody ever tried to come against her. Back in her day they called her "No Joke" because she *was* no joke.

When Tamal and Fancy first moved in she took pleasure in baking them an apple pie and welcoming them to the neighborhood on Philly's south side. Soon after, she realized they had issues. "Anytime you need a babysitter I'm right here for you," she told Fancy early on. "I know how hard it is to put up with a drunk." Mrs. Greenwire told Fancy about one of her last times with her husband.

"There was a knock at the door, and I allowed the men in blue to retrieve my intoxicated husband from the sofa," she recalled. "I told them to be my guest and take his ass before I bust him in the face again. I wouldn't allow any man – husband or not – to put his hands on me. Do you understand

Fancy? You don't have to go through that unnecessary crap either, even if he is your husband or your baby's father. That was last time I took abuse from George Greenwire. A few years later we were officially divorced."

Mrs. Greenwire sat down in her living room, staring out the window. *Good for Fancy. She got out in time...*

Chapter 7

SASHA

A couple of years after Fancy's disappearing act, Sasha grew immune to the emptiness in her heart. *I had a sister/cousin for only a couple of years, and now I'm lonely again in this doggone room. It's time for a change.* Tamal and Sasha had their good times and bad times. Tamal broke the news to her that he was moving over the bridge a week after Fancy bruised her heart with the same news. Yet never in her wildest dreams did she think they were an item, a couple, much less seriously dating.

Sasha already knew the day would come when Tamal would be ready to bounce. Tamal had lived with the Jackson family secret long enough and she couldn't blame him for wanting to leave Camden. Still, she knew she'd miss her best buddy.

Once again someone else has left my life, she reflected. "First it was my dad, then my Aunt Mary, next Fancy and now you. How can this keep happening to me, Tamal?" He couldn't answer immediately because he'd just had taken a bite of his chicken cheese steak.

"Huh, Tamal?" Sasha snapped impatiently.

"Aw, Sash, I'm going only right over the bridge to the Legacy Casino," he replied. It's not too far at all and you can come visit me anytime you want." Tamal extended the invitation knowing full well Sasha couldn't stand Pennsylvania.

"No, that's fine. I'll stay right here in my city and represent. All of you fake wannabe's keep leaving so who's going to hold it down here?" Sasha raised her eyebrow at Tamal while waiting to hear his response. He wiped some mayonnaise from his lip before speaking again.

"Sash, I got to try to make a better living for me," he said. "There's nothing here but partying, and I'm tired. We're getting older and we need to figure out what to do with ourselves." The whole time Sasha was congratulating him she wished she had the heart to make a big power move like Tamal and Fancy, who moved to Philadelphia to better themselves.

"That's great, Tamal. I'm so proud of you," she said. "You finally decided to be a dealer, huh?"

"Yea, Sash. It's about that time for me to get my own car, crib and to have a few dollars in the bank. Remember, anytime you want to get away you're always welcomed to come visit after I get myself together."

"Oh you know I'll be right there beating your couch up," she replied with a frown. "You know I owe you after all those years you tore up my mom's couch." They both giggled and finished their lunch at Corrine's Soul Food, one of the best places in town to chow down.

After a year passed Sasha had gotten used to being lonely, but that didn't stop her from partying and getting her groove on. She also went on several dates but eventually stopped dealing with Figga Ma Jiggas, her word for men. Instead, she decided to wait on the right man to bounce her way. Sasha no longer wanted to be stimulated in bed only. Forget all that sticking and licking. Any man coming her way from now on must also stimulate her mind. Sasha had finally gotten on her grind and gotten a job at the coffee shop on the corner of Haddon Avenue.

It was Sasha's day off and she wanted to take a stroll in her favorite, heavily worn sandals, but she was having trouble finding them. She decided to search Brenda's room, which she knew was a big no-no.

"Mom!" Sasha screamed furiously as Brenda rushed into her room.

"What is it baby girl?" Brenda asked without a clue.

"I found this under your bed," Sasha said while standing in the middle of her mother's bedroom with two wrinkled letters in her hand.

"Why are you going through my things, Sasha?" Brenda asked angrily. "I've told you plenty of times to stay out of my damn room. Nothing in here belongs to you. I'm a grown woman and you need to be respectful of my things."

"Mom, you're right, and I'm leaving this house sooner or later and you'll never have to worry about me again," Sasha said. "All you are is a liar. You lied about my dad and now you're lying about Fancy."

"Sasha tone your voice down with me young lady," Brenda shot back. "I'm not one of those girls back in high school that you used to fight. I'm Brenda Marie Rusty, and in case you've forgotten I'm the mother here." Sasha calmed down quickly after she realized Brenda was as serious as a heart attack. She knew Brenda could easily knock her from one side of the room to the other. After all, she'd heard plenty of stories about her mom on the city streets of Camden.

Sasha had heard all the stories. Your mom is no joke, one person told her. Another told her of a time Brenda smacked the wig off a woman during a fight and kept her face down in the mud at least a good 30 seconds. The part of Sasha that doesn't take any bullshit off anyone came from her mother.

"All right, mom. I just wanted to know why you lied about Fancy and her pregnancy?"

"Sasha, remember I'm a grown ass woman, and I don't have to answer to anyone," Brenda said. "You need to understand that, so please do not come at me with any more questions." The anger was apparent on Brenda's face, but so was the hurt because she knew Sasha now knew the truth about her father.

Sasha excused herself from her mother's bedroom just as Brenda tried to swing on her. *I knew that whench was going to try to hit me. I'm grown now and I can kick her ass.*

"Mom, I'm not a little girl anymore," Sasha warned her. "You can't beat me or make me your slave now." Brenda knew she couldn't handle Sasha and she had no right to put her hands on her anymore. But she also knew Sasha made a smart move by escaping out of her bedroom while she still had a chance. *Sasha would probably win the fight,* Brenda thought, *but she'd suffer some lumps and bruises in the process.*

"May I help you?" Sasha asked the tall dark-skinned fellow who was holding a newspaper in his left arm and pointing with his right hand.

"Yes, please. May I have a large espresso with extra sugar, beautiful?" Sasha had very fair honey-colored skin, was 5'2" with voluptuous hips and thighs and wore a size C bra, but she still didn't like this old man calling her beautiful. *Who the hell are you calling beautiful?* she thought. *You'd better step to left.* One thing Sasha couldn't stand was for old men to flirt with her. She ignored the man's comments and simply served him his beverage.

"One large espresso coming right up," Sasha said in a pleasant voice. "That'll be $2.28." She smiled as she gave the man his hot beverage and 82 cents change. As the old man walked away Sasha was just about to look up and greet the next customer when she heard a familiar voice.

"Sasha Rusty, your mother told me I could find you here," he said. "Now what made you humble yourself and get a job at the café?" Sasha's eyes widened as she looked at Tamal for the first time in a long time.

"Hey Tamal, how are you doing?" she smiled. "I've been calling you. Why haven't you been returning my calls?"

"I've been busy, girl. That Legacy got me as tired as hell," Tamal said while glancing at his cell.

"Word, you're making that paper," Sasha said while wiping down the counter.

"Hell yea, but there's a lot of bull crap you have to put up with. Trust me. That place of business is not for you, Sash."

Tamal, I'm really thinking about crossing that bridge, Sasha thought to herself. Just as she was about to say it to Tamal the woman who was next in line cleared her throat to get her attention.

"Oh, I'm sorry, Ms. May I help you?" Sasha asked before telling Tamal to find a table since she got a break in five minutes. As she got the lady's order she asked Tamal whether he wanted anything.

"Nah, I'm good. I'll be sitting over there in the corner," Tamal said while pointing at a two-seat booth in the corner near the jukebox. Sasha waited on her last customers before joining Tamal to catch up on old times.

"It has been some years now Tamal," Sasha said fumbling in her pocket.

"I know, and a lot has changed over the years," he said. Tamal knew it was time to tell Sasha that Krina was looking for her. He knew it was his fault for falsely putting the blame on her. He knew Sasha was clueless about Krina's hatred toward her and that she wanted to retaliate against her.

"Sash, how have you been?" Tamal hesitated, paying no attention to his convictions. "I've been fine just trying to save some dough so I can get out of my mom's crib," Sasha answered. "She's been bugging lately. And you won't believe this, but I found two letters she has been keeping secret from me. In one letter I read my cousin was pregnant before she left here and moved to Philly."

"Word?" Tamal said with a surprised look on his face. *Damn, it's like Sash knows what I'm thinking,* Tamal thought as his heart began racing. *Another secret I've got to soon disclose, that I'm the father of Fancy's baby.*

"I don't care to talk about the other letter right now," Sasha lowered her head in disappointment. "Hey Tamal, is Legacy anything like the reality show 'Trapped Dealers?' I've been watching that show since its first season and I'm hooked," she said, changing the subject. "Boy oh boy there be some stuff going on up in there. Last week's episode was about this dealer who was stealing money. He kept slipping purple chips into his sleeve on the roulette table and a player snitched on his ass. I don't know why the player did that because I would have told the dealer he had to split with me or else I'd tell and that's real talk," Sasha said, grinning.

Tamal ignored Sasha's excitement over wanting to know about the happenings at Legacy Casino. Instead, he reached for his cell phone and flashed a picture in her face.

"Who's that cute little boy with sexy eyes?" Sasha leaned over and asked.

"That's my son, Baby Tamal. He's 3 about to turn 4."

"What, by Krina?" Sasha asked with a puzzled look on her face.

"Naw, after our last talk before I left and took off over the bridge I took your advice and broke it off with Krina. Then I started smashing Trina a month later."

"What!!! Trina... her sister?" Damn, man."

"Yea, Sash. I took your advice. You said I should have been with Trina instead of Krina."

"Boy, I meant your first choice should have been Trina instead of Krina only because she already had a baby," Sasha clarified. "So you mean to tell me you had a baby by Trina? I don't even remember her being pregnant." Sasha was confused.

"Girl, no. I dealt with Trina for only a month because Krina whipped her ass three times and that's when I made a decision to leave Trina alone. They're twins and there was no need to come between them."

"Yea, you realized that after you banged them both," Sasha said sarcastically. How convenient. Have you bumped into Fancy out there in the City of Brotherly Love?"

"I used to see her but not anymore. Sash, that's what I came to tell you." At that very second Sasha's cell phone vibrated, indicating her break was over. "Well, Tamal, it was nice seeing you. I've got to go. My break is up. Answer your phone when I call you." They embraced and exchanged light pecks on the cheek.

Tamal failed once again to warn Sasha about Krina wanting to get at her simply because he had lied on her. And Krina really believed it was Sasha's fault Tamal dumped her right before he left for Philly because he used Sasha as his scapegoat. Nevertheless, he didn't tell Sasha his son was her little cousin. Tamal was acting like a typical, no-good man, trying to cover up his child. Deep down he knew God was watching him, and God doesn't like ugly.

Chapter 8

BREAK-ROOM

"Yo' Braze, what's up?"

"Nothing Tamal how's everything?"

"Man, these players are wrecking my nerves every 30 seconds," Tamal said. "This old Indian dude kept banging on the table and slobbering all over himself while wising out loud for 21. I thought to myself, man, every hand won't be 21."

"Tamal, you know the gamblers have issues, and if Leona was right here right now she'd throw one of her scriptures at you. Hold up; let me see if I can think of one. If the son makes you free, you should be free indeed. John 8:36 Yea, that's it!" Braze couldn't believe she actually remembered a scripture.

"Look out. Now we have Leona number two at Legacy," Tamal shouted.

"Stop playing, Tamal. I'm not nearly as bad as Leona," Braze responded. "She talks about Jesus all day long. I mean, she's my good friend and all, but she really leaves all her worries in His hands. I don't understand how she does it."

"I know. My mom is like that. She lets God handle all of her situations and that's why she and I have a rocky relationship now," Tamal said. "She said God would help my oldest sister, which he didn't."

"Oh, what happened to her, Tamal?"

"I'd rather not talk about it," Tamal said, changing the subject. "What type of players do you have today, Braze?" he asked while waiting for his Snicker bar to drop from the vending machine.

"Oh, my players are excellent and they tip very well," Braze sang. "I have one young black girl that keeps texting every two minutes and we have to keep reminding her to give a hand signal. Then I have an Asian couple that's constantly in conversation and I have no clue what they're saying. And on the end of my blackjack table there's an Indian guy who's very quiet and a chain smoker, but I don't mind."

"You never mind do you?" Tamal questioned. Everybody knows Braze Carter was a company woman. No matter how bad the tokes or players were she always found a way to make it sound like the place was better than it was and not an awful place to work.

"Braze, your players sound like they're annoying as hell, just like mine," Tamal said. "Well they're not, Tamal, and wipe that chocolate off your face."

Once again break time flew by. They all glanced at the clock then started walking briskly back to their tables.

One thing you shouldn't do was be late for the next dealer because dealers looked forward to getting their 20-minute break each hour. They needed their rest time because dealing on the casino floor broke you down emotionally and mentally. There once was a Legacy dealer who developed carpal tunnel in both hands. So it was very important for dealers to have break time. No matter the circumstances, if you were late for that dealer's break you should apologize and make it your business to be early for that dealer's next break to make up for the time he or she lost from the last break.

"Tamal and Braze are always late when they're on the same break," dealer Rayne said to J.T.

"Man, I know," J.T. said smiling.

"But when they're on the break with Leona, their asses be on time," Rayne shouted.

"Aw, they didn't mean any harm and they'll make it up on the next break I betcha," J.T. said, extending his hand to Rayne to see if she would shake it.

"Man, I'm not betting you. It's bad enough our tip rate is down and I don't have any damned money as it is. All my bills are due, so I don't think I want to bet on whether Braze and Tamal will be late from their break the next go round."

The noise during dealer breaks was virtually indescribable. The dealers in the break room continued having their loud conversations, and it sounded like a high-school cafeteria. Everyone was engrossed in a personal conversation, yet it became a whole new ballgame when Sasha Rusty joined the staff at Legacy because she said what every dealer only dreamed about saying.

Chapter 9

BRAZE

"Hey, hey, hey," Braze said as she quickly jumped from the sunken couch, leaving a face print on her pillow.

"What's all this noise about? You two need to be a little quieter because mommy just fell asleep a couple of hours ago."

"Mom, if you sleep in your room you wouldn't be able to hear the noise." Cindy slipped and said.

"Brody and I just want to know are you and daddy breaking up." Cindy shot the second question at her before giving Braze a chance to answer the first. Braze tied her robe, walked to Cindy and looked directly in her eyes.

"First of all young lady, do not speak to me in that tone of voice ever again," Braze said. For a while now she felt as though her parental grip was slipping, especially with Cindy. Braze knew how important it was for her kids to respect her, which was why she pondered what she was supposed to do. She was tired of living a lie, tired of fronting with her children. Still, sometimes telling a lie was much easier. "Your daddy and I are fine," Braze said, and as soon as we upgrade to a king-sized bed I'll be back sleeping in the bedroom with him. You know mommy's kind of on the heavy side." Cindy glanced at Braze and thought about Mr. Rogers, who was famous for telling stories. Meanwhile, Braze mistakenly thought she had her children fooled.

"Mom, dad told us a few nights ago y'all bed is king-sized and we helped him change the linen on your bed," Brody blurted out. "Cindy asked why he always had to order the sheets, and daddy said it was an unusual king-sized bed made in Italy."

"Oh shut up, Brody," Cindy said. "Mommy has been trying to sell us dreams for the last couple of months now." Cindy may be a teenager, but she had a clever mind and caring heart and felt her daddy's pain.

"Cindy, why and when did you start getting a smart mouth?" Braze asked in exasperation. "After school young lady you and I will have a talk. But for now you two run along before you miss the bus." Braze stormed upstairs to her bedroom, not believing how much mouth Cindy had.

"Jott, do you know Cindy has a smart mouth? Braze screamed as she walked into her bedroom to find a perfectly made bed. *Where in the hell is Jott,* she thought while looking all around the room. Braze checked in the huge walk-in closet, the powder room and their oversized master bath but found no sign of Jott. Then she spotted an envelope on her ottoman, where she did her daily reading. Braze moved her book, "Strawberry Letters," so she could sit and read the letter.

Dear Braze, I decided to stay at my mother's house for a few days. I know you have to go to work tonight, so I've arranged for my sister Jane to look after the children. Hopefully after we spend a few days apart we can work this thing out if you're willing. Braze, it's time to get married. I love you with my all my heart and soul. There's just

no way I see myself living without you. Yet you make it so hard for me to be good to you. I recall your friend Leona saying we need to get married real soon. The more we live in sin, the more sadness we'll endure. I will give you all the time you need to think about our future. But for now, take this time to fix the issue you have within yourself because I truly want to repair our broken home.
p.s. I LOVE YOU. Jott Stagger

Braze fell to her knees and started asking God to forgive her wrong doing and make her life better. Then she had a flashback of her mother telling her she would disown her if she married that white man, referring to her high school sweetheart Jott. So instead of being strong and standing up and being her own woman, Braze turned to her boss for advice and answers, which lead to their sexual relationship. In this moment she felt much shame for allowing her emotions to potentially destroy her future.

Chapter 10

TAMAL

T amal was enjoying the hot and steamy bath, soaking his Hershey-toned back. *Man, where's Leona when you need her? She picked a bad week to be on vacation,* he thought as he relaxed. Leona's words played over and over in his head as he sat in the tub: *Just remember to put God first in your life and everything else will follow.* The splashing sound of his soap hitting the bath water zapped thoughts of Leona out of his mind. She reminded Tamal a lot of his mother, but he needed her to understand what he was going through. Both women always tried to preach a good word to him, which was fine. But neither of them had taken a walk in his shoes. Tamal still couldn't see his son, but he was required to pay child support. He never had a good relationship with his parents, but he felt the love Leona gave him was sisterly like. *Thanks but no thanks for your Godly advice, sis,* Tamal thought as he dried off with his polo towel and took a sip of vodka while slipping into his cream Ralph Lauren boxers. *Who needs Godly advice when I've got Grey Goose,* he arrogantly thought.

Rrrring, Rrrring. Tamal pushed the pillow from his face, wiped his eyes and noticed the clock said 9 a.m. Who can be calling me this early in the morning, he mumbled.

"What's up?" he answered groggily.

"Tamal, that's how you answer the phone for your mother?" Mrs. Naydine Jackson snapped.

"Sorry ma. My bad" he said.

"It's your bad all right...your father is in the hospital..." Tamal tried to interrupt by saying "Ma, you," but Mrs. Jackson wasn't going to be outtalked this time.

"Tamal, you be quiet for once. I'm speaking. Your father is bad off. Now enough is enough. You ran off over the bridge and we haven't seen you since. I've forgiven you because it's been several years now. But at every family event everyone asks for you. Your Uncle Bud keeps asking me about his favorite nephew when he calls here. Now your father loves you more than anything and he's so sorry for what he did. The whole family has forgiven him, so why can't you come and pay him a visit in Cooper Hospital? I believe he's on his death bed at this very moment, son. He's dying from cancer. Now I must get back in the hospital room because I'll stay with my husband until he takes his last breath."

"Ma, I'll think about it," Tamal said angrily.

"Tamal, I did my part. It's time for you stand up and be a man," Momma Naydine said.

"Before you hang up, ma, let me ask you whether you told dad to stand up and be a damned man." Tamal hung up the phone without giving his mother a chance to answer, rolled over and went back to sleep.

Why is my sister screaming like that? "Mom, dad, tell Kymbah to shut her mouth. I have a basketball game tomorrow and it's 3 a.m.," Tamal shouted. He walked down the hall rubbing his eyes and screaming his older sister's name. "Kym, Kym, what's wrong?"

Just then Tamal saw his father dash back into his bedroom, but Tamal continued walking to Kym's room to ensure she was all right.

"Kym, are you all right?" When Tamal noticed she was bleeding from her genital area he shouted for his mom as loud as he could.

"Ma, Maaaaa, Mommmmaaaaa...," he yelled while cradling his sister and assuring her their mother, Naydine, would make their dad pay.

"What is it, Tamal, and why aren't you in your own room?" Naydine looked at her sweet, innocent daughter and noticed it looked like she'd been crying for dear life. "Boy, what have you done to your sister?" Naydine snapped.

"Momma I didn't do anything," Tamal cried. "I heard Kymbah screaming, and I saw daddy run out of her room like a madman back into your room. Then I found her like this." Tamal tried desperately to convince his mother he had nothing to do with Kymbah's state. He pleaded with her to believe him.

"Boy, how dare you blame this on your father? One more outburst like this and I'll send you to your Uncle Bud," Naydine threatened. Her brother was a tough guy in The Army for 10 years and would straighten Tamal out for sure if she sent him to stay with him. For the next eight years Tamal kept the Jackson family molestation a secret, except for confiding in his best buddy Sasha. He told her when he was 14 that his sister was molested by his dad during one of his drunken stupors. Tamal told Sasha he'd despised his father with a passion since he was 10. He said he had so much rage in his heart if he could have killed his father and gotten away with it he would have.

A few weeks later Sasha asked Tamal to go with her to his father's funeral. Tamal told her to get real. As far as he was concerned, his father needed to rot in hell for what he did to his sister, his own daughter, his own flesh and blood. Sasha reminded Tamal of what Leona would say: God is the judge. Tamal made it very clear he was the judge right now and he would not be attending his father's funeral.

"How's Tamal?" Naydine asked Sasha after the service. "He's fine. He has a great job and his own place."

"Well Sasha, you know I'm very grateful to you for showing up and paying your respects on Tamal's behalf. I sent him a suit and all and he still didn't show up."

"Don't mention it, Mrs. Jackson. It was a beautiful homegoing and Chennita, that girl can really sing!" Mrs. Jackson walked toward the black limousine and nodded her head in agreement.

"Yes, Chennita is one of the best, and tell your mother I said thanks for her bomb macaroni-n-cheese." Naydine paused before bending her head to get into the limo. "One more thing, Sasha."

"Yes," Sasha replied with sadness.

"Tell Tamal I'm so sorry and I love him."

"I sure will tell him," Sasha said.

The Jackson family secret is now dead. Can Mrs. Jackson really be that naive? Poor Kymbah, Sasha thought in sorrow.

Chapter 11

SASHA

N o. *Not again. They're doing another layoff? They just had one last season.* Sasha was so engrossed in the "Trapped Dealers" reality show. In fact, she considered it the most real reality show on television. Everything dealers went through in the industry she was able to watch on her 32' Sony. She assumed the next episode would be overwhelming, though she couldn't grasp why they laid off Brad the supervisor, the show's leading man. She tried to figure out how they could just lay him off like that, after he'd put in so many years with the company and never called out or was late. *Yo, this show is getting more like real life,* Sasha thought as she leaned forward to grab some popcorn, which she washed down with a glass of Sutter Home White Zinfandel. Rrring. Rrring. Aw hell, who's calling while I'm watching my show, Sasha said as she reached over the arm of her white leather couch for the phone. She glanced at the caller ID before picking up the receiver. The name read Braze Carter. Sasha knew she had to answer or Braze would continue blowing up her phone. Braze knew this was Sasha's night to be entertained by her favorite reality show, but she dialed her digits anyway. "Hello, Braze, one of my favorite co-workers. How can I help you this evening," Sasha said sarcastically.

"Hey! Sasha. Girl I just wanted you to know I decided to take your advice and I'm watching 'Trapped Dealers' tonight.

Grrrl…it's better than Legacy. Did you see that player whip out his manhood and pee-pee right there near the slot machine?" Braze said excitedly, talking a mile a minute. Sasha couldn't believe that Braze, the ultimate company woman, was watching a 'Trapped Dealers' episode. Truthfully, she was shocked. After realizing she and Braze had something in common besides working together she continued the conversation. "Yes girly, and that security guard turned his head the other way like he didn't see it," Sasha said while putting the last kernels of buttered popcorn in her mouth.

"Girl, what are you doing watching my show?" Sasha asked with enthusiasm, as if she was the producer.

"Every now and then I drop in on it," Braze said. "It's very interesting to see someone finally do a show on our industry. Anyway, girl I just called to ask if you can switch start times with me next Saturday."

"I'm not sure, but I'll let you know before Thursday although on the real I really don't even want to work Saturdays anymore after that damn player pooped in his pants and continued playing and not one damn supervisor escorted him out," Sasha said.

"Eeew, that's nasty, but his money spends, Sasha, and that's what counts at Legacy," Braze said in defense of the casino.

"*Oh shut the hell up company woman,*" Sasha thought before asking whether Braze had a hot date on Saturday. Sasha had already figured out Braze's scheme. She always tried to get a 6 p.m. start so she could spend extra time with their boss. Braze always had Jott believing she got off at 4 a.m. What Sasha didn't know was Jott had been sleeping at his mother's house for months.

"Well let me know. See you at work, Sasha." Braze hung up the phone faster than you could flip a light switch. Sasha felt as though Braze didn't give her a chance to say goodnight, but she knew it was late and she had a lot of running around to do in the morning so she really didn't care. Center City was crazy busy with tourists this time of the year. She called it a night right there on her uncomfortable leather sofa.

Let's go back a year and find out how Sasha got her own crib and became such good friends with Braze and Leona. Thanks to Tamal's guilty feelings he repaid Sasha with a favor despite second guessing himself.

After Sasha got bailed from jail and lost her job at the coffee shop she paid Tamal a visit. She was so hurt over him lying on her, which ultimately forced her to get into a fight with Krina, that she hopped a train to Philly to let him know how she felt. Sasha didn't know where Tamal lived but figured sooner or later she'd run into him or Fancy. She had often wondered after all these years why Fancy hadn't brought her little cousin to visit her. Sasha believed in her heart Fancy kept in touch with her mother because every time she mentioned Fancy's name Brenda always said, "Don't worry about Fancy, Sasha. You need to get yourself together." Sasha took heed to what her mother kept drilling into her thick skull. She prayed she would run into Fancy so she could get a full understanding of the situation between her and Tamal – and have more information than what she read in the letter she found in her mother's room. As Sasha rested her head on the seat of the train she noticed a fine brother who kept winking at her. She felt she had nothing to lose so she winked back.

"What's up, Sasha?"

"Hey, how are you?" Sasha removed her belongings from the train and *wondered who the hell is this guy and how does he know my name?* She tried to figure out who he was while walking faster and faster down Market Street, clueless about her destination. She was sure of one thing: Tamal worked the swing shift at Legacy over on South Street.

"Wait up, Sasha. Why are you walking so fast?" the stranger asked. He was very attractive, about 6′ 1″. He wore blue jeans with his belt around his waist like men are supposed to wear their pants, and a yellow striped button-up shirt with a blue fitted cap. *I'm telling you right now God if this man tries to hurt me I'm going back to jail, only this time for a lengthy sentence* Sasha said to herself repeatedly. After the man finally caught up with her she asked him why he was following her and how he knew her name. She hated her car had broken down, forcing her to hop on the train.

"Sasha, you dropped your ID on the train," the tall buttercream complexion man said politely. "Oh thanks. I really should have paid more attention to my property," Sasha giggled. "By the way, what's your name since you're already familiar with mine?" Sasha's flirty smile appeared, just as quickly as her panties moistened.

"My name is Damon. How do you do?" he said while extending his hand. "I'm good. Are you familiar with this area?" Sasha wondered why she went against her better judgment and began spilling the beans to Damon. She told him the reason she came to Philly was to find her best buddy/childhood friend, Tamal, and her favorite sister/cousin, Fancy. Damon invited Sasha to live in his home in north Philly, and even though she didn't know him from a can of paint, she accepted his invitation. In the back of her mind she wouldn't stay with him long, but after he started asking for sexual favors in exchange for rent, she knew it was time to bounce. She just kept praying and hoping she would soon run into Tamal or Fancy.

After two weeks passed and she hadn't run into either one of them, she knew it was time to start searching again. She decided to go back to Legacy to find Tamal but once again had no luck. Every time she went by he was off, he'd left early or called out sick. She couldn't understand the concept of his job until much later when she began walking in his shoes.

"Babes, you want to go to Club Gotham tonight?" Damon asked.

"Yea. Why not. I'm feeling like I can get my groove on tonight." Sasha really didn't want to go clubbing or anywhere else with Damon. Don't get it wrong. She enjoyed the shelter and the love making, but after he told her to kneel down and slob his manhood she was too finished. She figured there was no way she was going to put her thick lips on his uncircumcised manhood. *He got to be out of his cotton-picking mind. If he wants me to perform oral sex, I'm out.* Sasha started thinking about "escaping" from Damon's crib around the same time he got mad and told her he wanted her out if she couldn't perform sexual favors for rent. At that moment she realized she could use the club as her outlet.

"I'm hanging with my boys tonight and want you to be my designated drive because I'm planning on getting fucked up for my boy Tyron's birthday." Sasha couldn't stand Tyron either because he once had the nerve to brush against her backside without saying excuse me. Sasha knew it was a set up, and Tyron just wanted to know how far he could go with her. Next it would have been her breasts and after that a peck on the cheek until finally his mission was accomplished. Men used signals as a way to get to the panties, but Sasha killed his dream after his first slick move.

"Man, you got me twisted. I belong to Damon," Sasha said, lying. It hurt her to even say that, but she had to given the circumstances. "You two are best friends so don't try anything stupid." Tryon knew exactly what he was doing, and he knew he was dead wrong, but just like any other man he was trying to see how far Sasha would allow him to go. Nonetheless, Tryon quickly apologized after Sasha's outburst. "Oh my bad... Sasha. I didn't mean anything by it," he said while quickly moving away from Sasha. Right then and there Tryon knew she wasn't from Philly. Philly chicks would have enjoyed the bumping and grinding and kept it moving.

"You want me to be your designated driver so you and your boys can chill?"

"Yea, that's the least you can do sassy Sasha," Damon said. "You're all laid up in my crib for free and won't use those juicy lips for my pleasure. So...hell yea I want you to be my designated driver in exchange for rent, bitch." Now Damon was shouting with authority.

"Fine. I'll do it just this one time," Sasha said, barely above a whisper. She couldn't believe she had to humble herself and keep her mouth shut, but she weighed only 140 pounds and Damon was much bigger and stronger than she was. Sasha kept imagining how she could undo the pool of bullshit she was drowning in and figured her next move would be her best move.

Chapter 12

BRAZE

B raze was feeling real guilty because she knew Jott didn't deserve to be disrespected like she was doing. She tried calling Leona because she knew Leona would give her some spiritual inspiration and love in her time of need, but unfortunately she got no answer from her cell or house phone. Braze called Tamal thinking he could give her some advice from a man's perspective, but his answering machine picked up, too. Brazed glanced at her phone and thought she was bugging. *Tamal has his cell phone off in the middle of the day.* She closed her Blackberry and threw it in her tan Coach bag. Braze couldn't take her mind off of Tamal's phone being off. Then she shook her ill feeling by thinking *maybe he got so intoxicated last night he turned his phone off by accident.*

For just a quick second Sasha crossed her mind, but she knew Sasha wouldn't have anything good to say. *Better you than me* would easily come from her sassy mouth, so Braze concluded it wasn't a good idea to call that out spoken chick.

Braze drove to the supermarket and kept coaching herself to snap into a mother/fiancé groove. She planned to cook the children a nice, hot meal, something she rarely did. The children were so used to Jott's cooking and eating dinner with him, but Braze wanted to cook early so they could have a family discussion before she left for work. Jott was a good man and Braze didn't deny that. He cooked, cleaned, washed clothes, walked the dog and took care of the children. Hell, he even did the grocery shopping. What else could a woman ask for? Braze tried to prove to herself she could be great mother instead of a workaholic, but she fell short once again. Not only did she worship Legacy; she also loved Ms. Ford.

Braze made a U-turn from the supermarket entrance soon as she walked in. She decided to leave the shopping to Jott and prayed he came back home soon. She knew grocery shopping wasn't her style even though she looked likes she loved to eat. She ate a lot of junk at Legacy, thus the extra pounds. Feeding her face when she was in distress caused her to gain weight, and as long as she could recall she had been in distress all her life. Braze drove down Broad Street and ordered fried chicken for the children instead.

She deposited her key in the door just in time to witness a smirk on Jane's face. Braze's smile turn upside down the minute she saw her soon-to-be sister-in-law. Jane is content – until you mess with her younger brother Jott. Braze felt uneasy about Jane being in her house without her permission. She took one look at Jane and felt steam vibrating off her body. Braze wanted to tell the white ho to get the heck out of her home so badly, but she needed her to babysit the children in a few hours.

"I really prefer your brother to be with the children, but since he's acting like a baby I guess you'll do because I can't imagine the children being home all hours of the night alone," Braze said.

"My sis. My sis, how are you?" Jane fiercely asked. "The feeling is mutual because I'd prefer my brother was here, too, instead of me. Maybe if you start giving him some nooky you wouldn't have to worry about him not being here." Braze was really amazed that Jott went to his mother's house and told his sister she wasn't sleeping with him. She wondered whether did he tell his mom.

"Now why would Jott tell you a lie like that? Braze replied in frustration.

"Hey sis, get serious. I've called my brother plenty of names but liar has never been one of them. Besides, what man in his right mind has to lie about you?" Jane stretched her hands out real wide as if she simulating a huge person. "You think he wants to run home and tell us *you're* not giving up the nooky? Shit. I'd deny that every chance I got. Face it, sis. You stopped loving my brother a long time ago, and I advise you to cut the switch short before someone gets whipped by it." Jane wanted to dig real deep to let Braze know who's the boss, but instead she listened to her mother's advice and gave it to Braze lightly for the sake of her niece and nephew.

Braze raised her head up at Jane, feeling smaller than Webster. She knew Jane was right and she didn't give it up like she used to. Well, not to her brother anyway. Braze was still trying to figure out how Jane could come in her house and talk smack to her. As small as she was Braze had at least 150 pounds on her. She didn't like it, but Braze applauded her fiancé's sister for stepping up as a woman.

"Wow Jane, you got spunk huh? I never saw this side of you," Braze said.

"Nobody ever sees this side until they fuck with my mother or my brother," Jane said.

"Well, he's my children's father but right now I just don't feel like making love or having quick sex after I get off work. I work from 8 p.m. to 4 a.m. and by the time I get home and get out of the shower I'm exhausted. Your brother doesn't understand how drained I am after working in that casino."

Jott had also told Jane that on Friday Braze usually got in the house around 5:15 a.m., so Jane asked her what that was about given it took only 10 minutes for her to drive home.

"Oh, that's nothing." Braze tried avoiding the question by placing the chicken in the microwave. *Ms. Ford is everything. She's tall, chocolate, pretty has a job and knows how to hold me,* she thought.

"Braze, Braze. Do you hear me talking to you? Are you just going to stand there in a daze? Yo, my brother wasn't kidding. You are in love with somebody else. It's written all over your face," Jane said after watching Braze's 10-second trance.

"Oh girl, I'm sorry. I didn't get too much sleep on the couch last night," Braze said once she came back to reality, totally ignoring the way Jane had just called her out.

"Have you ever considered calling out and just getting some rest?" Jane suggested. "If you call out for a few days I believe Legacy will still function. What do you think?"

"No, I'm not calling out. I have one more night to go then I'm off. I'll be just fine, and I really appreciate you for staying over."

Braze hoped Jott would be back home before the week was out, but if not she would have to break down and ask her mom to babysit. "I'm going to take a cat nap before work. Tell the children their dinner is in the microwave, and thanks again for helping out, Jane." Braze walked up the steps down the hallway and into her bedroom. She waved at Jane and closed her door.

Jane, meanwhile, had to keep her cool because she saw right through Braze's cheating, lying and conniving. Jane loved her brother dearly and wondered *how Jott could love the fat bitch.* She tried so many times to tell Jott he deserved a better woman than a snake in the grass who tried to act like Ms. Perfect while she was destroying her household over some outside nooky. Jane had had enough of Braze's lies. She hoped they never got married and Jott grew some real balls and left Braze for once and for all.

Just like women, men don't have to stay in unhealthy relationships. Many women have game, too. Men who are trying to do God's will and live right will eventually be blessed with good wives. And they shouldn't let children be the reason for staying in unhealthy relationships. Being a good father doesn't necessarily mean staying with no-good women just to live in the same home with the children. Apparently Jott didn't get – that or he was hopelessly in love.

Chapter 13

BREAK-ROOM

"This doggone player knew he didn't have a hard eight. Yet still, I asked him three times if he wanted his hard eight back. The man was so busy worrying about that nasty cigar and his drink 'til he never noticed he didn't throw his $25 back in for his hard eight. Now three rolls later a hard eight hit and he was screaming, asking where his money was," Sasha said. She told him he didn't have a hard eight, but her floor supervisor overrode her and told her to pay him for his hard eight anyway.

Sasha was so mad you could see fumes steaming from her ears. Even when she was explaining to Braze what happened she was still rolling her eyes and was fighting mad. Braze continued washing her hands while Sasha's hands moved all over the place like a clown doing a juggling act.

"You know Braze, I just don't get why in the hell they always do that," Sasha bellowed. "They know damned well the players are sick and are always trying to cheat. HE DIDN'T HAVE A DAMNED HARD EIGHT." Sasha screamed so loudly her voice echoed in the hollow bathroom.

"Players always think they're supposed to get their way in craps," she continued. "I tell them like this. Either you have the bet or you don't. I don't want to hear, 'I forgot it,' or 'You know I play it all of the time' when they didn't play it. But just let the number they usually play hit. Those same players will be expecting to get paid. You understand what I'm saying, Braze?"

"Uh, not really. I don't know anything about craps, Sasha," Braze said with a confused expression.

"I don't even know why I'm talking to you anyway because you're such a company lady," Sasha told her.

"No I'm not. I just don't believe in calling out from work, that's all," Braze countered in a low voice.

"Well, I'm going to call out every chance I get because they don't even grant me Saturdays off when I request them," Sasha pitched back in a much louder voice. As they left the ladies room and entered the break room Braze whispered into Sasha's ear like she was telling her something top secret.

"Sasha, you knew before you came to work for this industry that your social life would be limited. "Tamal, J.T. Leona and I warned you."

"No, Braze. *Your* social life is limited," Sasha retorted. "I'm still going to party, drink and bullshit around with my men and if they don't give me Fridays off so I can watch my favorite reality show I'll call the fuck out with no problem. Besides, I'm only a part-timer unlike you Braze. You're the one holding all the clout and making the big bucks."

Braze ignored the last comment.

"Sasha, why do you watch that stupid reality show anyhow?"

"Braze, I'm not like you. I don't get into all the wifely duties like cooking, cleaning, walking your dog Max and playing teacher with the kids while helping them with their homework." Little did Sasha know Jott was the one handling all of the so-called wifely duties.

"Well, I have a lot of time on my hands," Sasha said. "I have no children, no steady man by choice because they're all liars and cheaters in my book, and besides, the show reminds me of this damned place." Sasha moved a little closer to Braze and whispered in her earlobe, "I forgot you have the best of both worlds." Then she giggled before encouraging Braze to watch the next couple of episodes because Nina the dealer was having an affair with Dotty the floor person.

"Does that sound quite familiar, Braze?" Braze didn't reply and Sasha kept going. "If Dotty's husband Cliff finds out it's going down on Trapped Dealers next week." Now Braze simply wanted to hurry and get away from Sasha.

"Shoot. With all the affairs and cheating I've witnessed in this place, I'm telling you when Cliff finds out Nina's ass is grass," Sasha said.

"That's the stuff you like to watch in your spare time, bull crap reality TV shows. Don't you get enough of the casino scene? When I'm home I think nothing about this place," Braze said, lying through her gapped teeth.

"Oh, don't get it twisted Braze. I couldn't care less about this job and that's why I call out whenever I want. Meanwhile, you're always trying to get perfect attendance. Although I can relate to the show I watch it for entertainment purposes only, sweetie."

"Well, suit yourself Sasha. I have to get back on the floor because my break is over," Braze put her unfinished chips in her locker then paced back to the casino floor.

"My break is up, too. And now I have to deal with these complaining ass players for another hour. See you next break, Braze."

"Tamal, when I tell you that was the longest hour of my life, trust me," Sasha said. "I'm really starting to get sick and tired of craps. Just now this old white man who looked like he needed to be in a nursing home came to the table. His hands were shaking and he was talking real low. And Tamal you know we can barely hear with all of those slot machines and the music as it is. I asked him if I could help him and he caught an instant attitude and said he'll never come back to Legacy again. Sometimes I feel just like the women in 'The Help'. Those maids ensured everything was in order but everybody still treated them as if they were less than human. Some customers have no respect for us. Now I ask you, what type of craziness is that, Tamal?"

"Sasha, you're going to have to stop letting the players get you so upset," Tamal cautioned. "You already know they have issues just by the fact that they are regulars in this place. That show you love portrays our life so well I don't know why you're acting like there's something different going on up in here?"

"Hell yea, Tamal. That's my show. I'm counting the days 'til the new season airs. The producers of 'American idol' wish they had ratings as high as my show," Sasha said. She had been trying to get Tamal and Leona to watch it since last season, but Tamal said he didn't bring his job home, and Leona always wanted to preach the word.

"Man, I've missed Leona and her encouraging talks. How long is her vacation?" Sasha asked.

"She has a week left before she comes back to work," Tamal answered.

"I tried calling her but her answer machine came on immediately both times," Sasha said.

"What are you calling her for, for prayer?" Tamal joked.

"Oh shut up, boy. She said she would assist me on an idea of mine because she was working on a project herself," Sasha continued. "She believes Jesus is going to get her out of Legacy, and I believe He is, too, so I need to grab onto her coattail."

"Sasha, what are you talking about? You don't even go to church," Tamal enlightened her. "First you have to build a relationship with Jesus. Don't just think He solves all of your problems while you're still mixed up in your worldly affairs."

Tamal sounded like Leona, and all the dealers in the break room said simultaneously: "Let the church say *AMEN!*"

"Tamal, you've been talking to Leona too long. You sound just like a walking church," Sasha said. "I don't care if I have to work here. I'm only a part-time dealer. Three to four days a week aren't bad. Leona's the one who wants out so badly."

"Yea, because she has a family and she loves spending quality time with her husband and three kids," Tamal explained. "Lamont works normal hours as a lawyer and has weekends off. Leona just wants the same thing, that's all. Is there anything wrong with that Sasha? Tamal quickly glanced at the clock.

"Naw, Tamal. You're right. I guess all of our lifestyles are different. Hey Tamal if you're not doing anything come over Friday and check out the new season of my show because it's going to be off the hook."

"I'll pass, Sasha. I saw one episode last year and some dealer named Angie smacked the shitout of a player because he bucked at her like he was going to hit her. She didn't even get in trouble. If that happened here you know damned well somebody would get fired."

Sasha interrupted Tamal and said, "Angie is my girl. Yea, they didn't fire her. That's what's up. All she was doing was defending herself. Fair is fair." Now Sasha was jumping and dancing like she was celebrating Angie smacking that player.

"I know you really like that show, Sasha, but for real it's a bunch of nonsense," Tamal said, throwing his hands in the air in disgust. He glanced at the clock for the last time and noticed they had only five more minutes before they had to go back on the floor.

"No, it's not a bunch of nonsense. Well, maybe to you it is. We all see what's going on everyday in this business. That show just makes us see ourselves and how dense we are. The Legacy treats us any ole kind of way. I like the show and I can't wait until Friday."

Break time was up, and all the dealers dashed back onto Legacy's gaming floor.

"See ya, Sasha!" Tamal said as he waved goodbye.

Thirty minutes later Sasha was soaking in madness. She was talking to every dealer in the Legacy break room. She had one hand on her hips and pointed with the other.

"Listen up, dealers. I know all us are getting sick and tired of being sick and tired, so we need to do something about it. This damned lady was just on my game and called me a bitch. Sasha had asked for a bathroom break because she was at her wit's end and needed to get away after that last episode. Sasha knew she was supposed to be on her game, but instead she was in the break room gossiping.

"Girl, calm down. We're all going through it on that casino floor. I just had a player wipe his snot with his hands and then he expected me to change his money," Rayne said.

"Well did you, Rayne?" Sasha asked sarcastically.

"Yes, I changed his money, but as soon as came in here I washed my hands."

"Oh no. I wouldn't have changed that money, at least not until they gave me some hand sanitizer for his nasty ass," Sasha said. It's just like on 'Trapped Dealer's when Chris was in that same situation and he called his supervisor Rohakemma over. He told her to give him some wet wipes before he touched that player's money.

Sasha thought she knew it all, but she went through some of the same things as the rest of her co-workers.

"I have this other player on the left side of me. Every time he shoots the dice he has to lick his hands. I told my box man

Rashad that I'm going to skip his shoot the next go around if he doesn't say anything to that finger-licking player."

Ms. Marlin interrupted and told Rayne, "Just keep some hand sanitizer on you, baby. And don't listen to Sasha. If she keeps following that reality show she's not going to have a job soon."

"Ok, ok, ok. We're all dumb, stupid and whatever else you want to call us in some sense, but the bottom line is we need a job and nobody else is offering us $20 or more an hour, so we just have to suck it up and take the bull crap," Rayne said, ending the conversation.

Many dealers turned to sordid activities on their days off, including drinking, gambling, smoking weed and cigarettes – all of which were bad. They also played the lottery hoping they could win big so they could quit working in casinos, which are very stressful places to work. People who had never been dealers should receive some type of counseling before trying to become dealers.

Chapter 14

SASHA

Once Sasha parked the car she and Damon went their separate ways as Damon looked at his cell to check the time.

"Sasha, it's 11:30. Come find me in two hours. The club lets out at 2 a.m., and I want to get a head start on the traffic. So let me chill with my boys tonight and you do your own thing." Sasha just looked at him, knowing he had no clue what she was up to. *Yea, I'm doing my own thing tonight brother, for real. And good riddance to you.* This was Sasha's night to make her power move, and she wanted to make a quick exit.

God, please send me an angel she thought as she nodded to Damon indicating she'd be back by 1:30 to get him. After an hour passed, Sasha glanced toward the bar and saw Damon and Tyron getting wasted. They looked like two drooling puppies, lusting over every woman that walked by them.

"Excuse me. Move." The two chicks bumped into Sasha as she pretended to be MacGyver on the dance floor, all the while keeping track of Damon's moves.

"My bad" Sasha said. *Not tonight, bitches. I'm on a mission.* On any other given night Sasha would have tried to demolish those Philly skanks, but tonight she simply maneuvered her way to the exit door. *This is my time to bounce from sex maniac and his crazy ass friend.* Sasha took one last look back to see if the dog catchers were looking her way. Surprisingly, she saw

her long-lost buddy, Tamal, leaning over the wooden bar with
several empty shot glasses lined up in front of him. The music
was bumping with the deejay playing old school songs,
Sasha's favorite kind. The floor was packed.

Biggie Biggie Biggie can't you see
Sometimes your words just hypnotized me
And I just love your flashy ways
Guess that's why they broke and you're so paid.

Sasha tried making her way over to Tamal, but on the way
while she was bouncing to the Notorious B.I.G. she notice
Damon's gloomy eyes were following her like Twitter. *I'm
going to rape that tonight,* Damon thought.   Sasha felt his
drooping eyeballs on her tush, so she made a quick U-turn
onto the crowded dance floor.

"Oh snap, this is my song," she exclaimed while Salt-N-
Pepper-n-Pepa played.
Express yourself, oh yeah oh yeah.
Let me be me.
Next the deejay played Sasha's girl, Mary J. Blige.
Real love. I'm searching for a real love. Sasha began singing
like she was MJB herself. The deejay switched songs and
Sasha's and Damon's eyes locked momentarily as another one
of her jams starting blasting across the sound system.

Fine, fine, fine, fine, fine, ooooh
Fine, fine, fine, fine, fine, ooooh.
Just fine fine, fine, fine, fine, fine, ooooh.
You see I wouldn't change.
My life, my life just fine

Before she realized it, Sasha had danced off of six songs in a
row. By the time she made it to the bar to get some water she
was all hot and sweaty. The number of empty vodka shot
glasses had grown, but Tamal was nowhere in sight.

Sasha tried to figure out where her intoxicated buddy Tamal had gone. She looked all around the club, even in the men's room. She knew he couldn't have gotten too far after drinking all of those vodka shots. By the time D.J. L-Boogie played Ja Rule as the last song Sasha was on her last leg.

Where would I be without you, uh?
I only think about you-yeah
I know you tired of being lonely, (lonely)
So baby girl put it on me

Sasha danced herself into a sweaty shower, drenching her clothes and hair. She had her shoes in her oversized pocketbook and plenty of holes in her stockings, but at that point she didn't care. All she wanted to do was find Tamal and get away from Damon as quickly as possible.

Sasha felt God had answered her prayers by letting her run into Tamal, despite his drunken state. When she finally located Tamal he was slumped over in the corner of the lounge. Sasha wanted to punch Tamal in his face for lying on her to Krina, but on the other hand she felt blessed to see him.

Sasha started dragging Tamal by his gray hooded sweat shirt. She glanced over at the bar and Damon and His boy was swapping numbers with the chicks in the lace outfits. Sasha didn't care. She was glad another woman had Damon's attention so she could make her get away.

"Get up, Tamal," she whispered with a hint of desperation in her voice.

"What are you digging in my pants for, Fancy?"

"*Fancy*. I'm *not* Fancy. I know everybody says we look alike but Tamal, you of all people know me. Now where is your car?" Sasha knew Tamal had been taking vodka shots but was still very surprised he called her Fancy.

Outside, she kept hitting the key alarm to Tamal's car like she was playing a video game. Eventually the alarm sounded.

"Oh, is *this* you?" Sasha asked while admiring Tamal's black on black Benz with 20-inch chrome rims. Ironically it was parked right beside Damon's black SUV.

"Give me your wallet," Sasha demanded as she continued shaking down Tamal's pockets like a cop performing a drug search. She needed his license to put his address into the vehicle's GPS because God knows she didn't know her way around Philadelphia and as drunk as he was she couldn't trust him to give it to her accurately. Once she found his license and read his address she became more excited because he lived on the opposite side of town from Damon. She knew that because she remembered a conversation in which Damon said it was easier for women to step across town and be accepted than it was for men. During that conversation Damon mentioned a few across-town streets by name, and Tamal just happened to live on one of them. So Sasha would move from north Philly to south Philly and never have to worry about Damon again – or so she thought.

Sasha walked toward Tamal's doorstep and was blown away by his townhouse. She admired his glass door with beautiful frame trimming as well as the red and brown bricks leading to his door.

Sasha wrestled with Tamal, who staggered badly, and finally managed to pull him into the house. *Oh wow! Tamal is definitely living the good life,* she thought once inside his crib. Sasha stepped back and quickly scanned his beautifully furnished townhome. If she had to guess she'd swear a woman had a hand in decorating. He had a dark chocolate suede sofa and a glass marble table centered in front of it. *Ebony* magazines lay neatly on the table.

The next morning Sasha and Tamal got caught up, and she told him all about her arrest after Krina busted up in the coffee shop ready to fight.

"Sash, I wanted to call you after I heard the news, but I was scared. You know how you are," Tamal said with sincerity. Sasha knew Tamal meant what he said, so she forgave him. He offered his place to her for as long as she needed to stay. Tamal felt he owed her big time so that was the least he could do.

"I'm not staying for long, but you have to put me on this dealer gig," Sasha said as she looked around Tamal's place and nodded to show how much she admired it.

"Sasha, you're not ready," Tamal said somewhat timidly. He knew Sasha had a temper and could go from zero to 60 in a matter of seconds.

"Hell yea I'm ready. I've been watching 'Trapped Dealers' for years," Sasha rebutted. "I can be like Mobetta. She takes no shit from anybody."

"Well, that's on TV. In the real world you have to smell it and you have to eat a lot of shit to stay in the industry and that's real talk, Sash," Tamal informed her. "Trust me. With your hyper attitude you won't last long in the business. I've seen a lot of people get fired over stupid stuff. Even if you're right Legacy always runs the show." Tamal spoke with emphasis because he needed his homegirl to fully understand what he was trying to convey to her.

"Tamal, once I was released from Camden County I had to pay a fine and I lost my job at the coffee shoppe," Sasha said. "I really wasn't making much, but thankfully I was living at home with my mom and was able to make ends meet. Then I got into a big fight with my mom after I found a letter Fancy wrote her saying she was moving to Philly with her soon-to-be baby's father." Tamal's face went blank. *Fancy never told me she told her Aunt Brenda about the baby.* Next his mind went blank. Tamal saw Sasha's lips moving, but he wasn't hearing a word she said. He also couldn't speak. Everything stopped after she said soon-to-be baby's father.

"Yo, Tamal. Do you hear me?" Sasha smacked her lips as she tapped his kneecap.

"Yea. I hear ya," he replied dishonestly.

"Well, anyway, the day Fancy left after we ate lunch at the mall some chick picked her up in a red Corvette," Sasha continued. "She must be conceited or something because her license plate read *It's Me*, like people are supposed to know what that means.

"Fancy told me she would be all right but never once mentioned being pregnant. So once again my mother lied."

"Well Sash, don't be too hard on your mom," Tamal said, now that he'd found his voice again. "You know we all have secrets."

"Tamal, shut up and let me continue my story," Sasha smacked her lips once more. "After that I packed my shit and caught the train as soon as I got released from Camden County." Sasha reminded him she really had come to Philly to kick his backside for putting her in the mix with the twins.

"Just like Myra did in 'Trapped Dealers.' She went straight to Craig's table and made a scene until the scary security guards escorted her out. I was coming for you in rare form. Then I got detoured by Mr. Damon."

"Who's Mr. Damon?" Tamal questioned.

"He's a story within itself. But it's my fault for being horny at the sight of a fine, muscle tone brother," Sasha admitted.

"Damn, Sash. I thought I was going through. My baby's mother tripped on me and moved out," Tamal said. "I'm very sorry about the twin's situation. Krina texted me that she was paying you a visit, but I didn't think it would lead to you going to county. I told her you said you didn't want me to date her only because she had a kid and her sister, Trina, didn't have any responsibilities."

"Oh, it's ok. I'm over that shit now," Sasha told him. "I do know she won't be ordering French Vanilla with whipped cream anytime soon." Sasha chuckled as she replayed the day in her mind.

"Yea, I got plenty of texts about that day," Tamal said with excitement. *[Sasha jus whipped ur gurl ass]- [Tamal, Camden is poppin. All I can say is French Vanilla baby]- [Hey, T, ur buddy Sash just burnt my sis. It's on.]- [Tamal, Sash is locked up].*

"I betcha she won't cross my path anymore over some bull," Sasha said in between giggles.

"Yo Sash, I told my boys I wasn't touching Camden grounds until I made peace with you. Hell, I didn't know if you had some hot chocolate for my ass," Tamal joked. They both chuckled as Sasha flicked channels.

"I miss our chats we used to have," Tamal said.

"Me too." Sasha really wanted to ask him why he called her Fancy after all the years they'd hung out together. Even through all of their many drunken episodes he'd never before mistaken her for Fancy.

"I'm really sorry if I caused you any harm, Sash. Can you ever find it in your heart to forgive me? And you know if there's anything I can do let me know, okay." Tamal still wasn't out of the clear because he didn't build up the courage to tell Sasha his son was her little cousin. It turned out they both were withholding information to protect each other's feelings.

Chapter 15

SASHA

Although it had been months now since Sasha kicked Damon to the curb, she was living in south Philly which seemed to be so much better than north Philly. Sasha enjoyed sitting out on Tamal's miniature porch watching the sun set. She started watering his plants and making light meals for them. She never told Tamal how proud she was of him but figured he could tell by the small favors and chores she did around the house. He had accomplished what he said he was going to, but one thing kept bothering her: She never got to meet his son. And where in the world was Fancy?

Rrring. Rrring. Sasha ran inside to answer Tamal's house phone. *It better be who I think it is.* She picked up the phone and said hello while fumbling with the cord.

"Can I speak to Sasha Rusty? a raspy voice asked.

"This is she." The sound of excitement in her voice let the person on the other end know she was waiting on this call. *Finally, my buddy Mally got me the hook up!* Sasha had been waiting for Jeff to call from Legacy for about a week. It appeared Tamal came through and pulled some strings for his buddy after all.

"How are you? I'm Jeff Ross from employee relations. I'd like to know if you're still interested in becoming a dealer here at Legacy." Sasha jumped for joy. "Yes, sir. I'm still interested," she said excitedly. She quickly asked Jeff when she could start. He gave her all of the information she needed and the rest was history. Not only did Sasha work for Legacy; she became a legacy.

After begging Tamal and promising him she would change her ways and not get him into trouble, Tamal took a chance on her. He felt somewhat guilty over her fight with Krina and subsequent arrest and knew he owed her big time. From all of the lying and trouble he caused, he felt getting her a job at Legacy and helping her get on her feet was the least he could do.

After working in Legacy for a while, Sasha realized why Tamal drank so much. Legacy took a toll on you while dampening and draining your spirit. Between the job and him being a deadbeat dad, the alcohol was Tamal's only comfort when he wasn't at work.

Tamal, this job is so much harder than the way it's portrayed on 'Trapped Dealers,' "

Sasha said. "I told you Sash. That's why I try to drink my job away every fucking chance I get."

Truth be told, Sasha really wanted to know how he worked so many years without being fired. She didn't think she'd make it past a year.

Tamal enlightened her. "Leona's prayers kept me going. She was the only true Christian sister walking in that devil's playground that was my friend." Leona had a habit of laying hands on her friends and praying for them at work. Sometimes other co-workers snuck to her and asked for prayer as well.

After receiving a couple of paychecks, Sasha moved into her own townhome in Tamal's complex. Sasha met Braze and

Leona, Tamal's friends who also pulled some strings to get her on at Legacy, and eventually she became good friends with them and thanked them for helping her. Sasha promised herself to keep her mouth shut, to an extent, so she could pay her bills and keep a roof over her head. She loved Tamal and their friendship, but in all honesty she was tired of his excessive drinking.

Why in the hell is he digging up his nose? Sasha was pissed because a player was digging for gold on her Blackjack table. She wanted to tell him to get the heck off of her table but thought about her MBs, her home, her car and decided against it. "Excuse me, sir. You'll have to get some tissue because I prefer not to catch any of your germs today." Sasha had a slick tongue and tried to use it to her advantage, but she knew she couldn't afford to get into any trouble. The Asian man wiped his nose and hands with the tissue a supervisor gave him.

"This is not my break now," Sasha replied after noticing she'd been dealing for only 40 minutes. Ms. Marlin, another dealer, told her she was wanted in the supervisor's office. Sasha knew sooner or later she would end up there, but this was sooner than she thought.

"What...for?" Sasha questioned. Ms. Marlin hunched her shoulder as she tapped on the Blackjack table.

"Hello, Ms. Ford. You wanted to see me?" Sasha's heart was racing.

"Sasha, you've been here for months now and I really have to make it clear that you are not allowed to ask for tips. This is a warning. The next time it will lead to termination. Do I make myself clear?" Ms Ford raised her voice just a tad while admiring Sasha's 34 C's peeking through her work shirt.

"Yes sir, I mean ma'm" Sasha gritted. With a silent giggle she left the office. *Oh, my bad. 'Mr. Her' and Braze need to be ashamed. She looks like a pimp and Braze looks like she needs to do a sleepover at Terri's Zumba. How do women do that nasty shit?*

After she left the office Sasha stopped to sign the E.O. list so she could leave early. She didn't feel like dealing to any more players after receiving her final warning. *How in the world will these players know I work for tips if I don't tell them? It was bad enough they started me off at $4 an hour.* She knew it was a bunch of bull. After watching "Trapped Dealers" all of those years she realized Legacy was nothing more than a cheap copycat.

Dear Aunt Brenda,

I'm writing you this letter to inform you that I'm three months pregnant by Tamal, Sasha's best buddy. We've been sneaking around behind Sasha's back because she's so over-protective of me and I know she would have tried to stop me from kicking it with him. We figured it was best to keep it hush-hush. Well, anyway we'll be moving together to Philly as soon as graduation is over. After I get settled in I'll call you. Better yet, I'll send you some pictures of my son. Yup. We found out we're having a baby boy. Please take this money and do something nice for yourself. My mother would have been so proud of you for stepping up and taking care of me as if I was your own...P.S. Give my love to Sasha and tell her not to worry so much about me. Fancy J. Rusty.

Sasha tried her best to figure out how to get in touch with Fancy without Tamal's help. She wanted to snap on Tamal so bad for sneaking around with her sister/cousin while also messing with other dizzy bimbos. No wonder he was so fast to take Fancy to the prom. She knew Tamal wasn't going to come clean that easily so she had to keep her composure. Sasha knew all of Tamal's grimy moves, but one day she planned to bust him in action. What Sasha didn't know was her bust was closer than she thought.

"Sasha, how about putting the tulips over there next to the daisies," Mrs. Greenwire said. "Sure, why not, Mrs. Greenwire." Sasha's back was to Mrs. Greenwire, who couldn't see her frown. "BINGO," Sasha shouted. There she was. Fancy Rusty, stepping out of her gold Camry. "What? Where is Bingo" Mrs. Greenwire shot back at Sasha. "I haven't been to Bingo since they took it out of our church."

You shouldn't be gambling up in The Lord's house in the first place, Sasha thought. *I do know that much.*

"Excuse me Sasha, did you say something?" Mrs. Greenwire asked.

"Oh, no. Mrs. Greenwire, just singing," she lied.

"Oh, okay dear. If that's what you call singing," Mrs. Greenwire said, smiling.

"Sasha, what are you doing sitting on my car? Get off now," Fancy screamed. "Now is that any way to greet your long-lost favorite sister/cousin?" Sasha asked as she jumped off Fancy's Camry.

The two women stood face to face as if they were about to kiss.

"Start talking, Fancy, or you won't be getting in this Toyota today."

"Look, Sasha, I had a long day at work helping my associate, Corvette, solve a case. Maybe we can do lunch at Ms. Tootsie's and I'll come clean about everything," Fancy bravely said.

"Fair enough, I need to get back over there to Mrs. Greenwire to finish helping her plant her flowers anyway."

"Mrs. Greenwire is truly a special lady. You know she reminds me of Aunt Brenda," Fancy said.

"Now that you mention it she has spunk like my mom, but Mrs. Greenwire is a big lady and I'd hate to get on her bad side. See ya tomorrow at Ms. Tootsie's around four o'clock," Sasha shouted as she ran back toward Mrs. Greenwire's front yard.

"You got it. Love ya," Fancy said as she drove off into the sunset. They never even noticed Tamal peeking out his curtains, and he never opened the door for Fancy. *What's love got to do with it,* he slurred.

"How many will be dining?" the young lady dressed in black asked. Sasha and Fancy replied two in unison. "This way, please." The young waitress led them to a table for two, handed them menus and took their drink orders before putting some hot, buttered cornbread on the table.

"Wow, Ms. Tootsie did her thang, Sasha mumbled as she stuffed a fork full of baked macaroni-n-cheese in her mouth. *I should smack the taste out of her mouth for lying to me and leaving me, but I love my cousin so let me hear her out first then I might smack her.*

"Yes, it has changed quite a bit since our moms used to drive us up here," Fancy responded. *I wish she would think about hitting me,* she thought, picking up on Sasha's vibe. *And right now she looks like she wants to fight.*

"Hmmm. These stuffed turkey chops are all that," Sasha said, licking the gravy off her fingers. She missed her mom's home-style cooking and was sick of the food at Legacy. The workers were treated like dogs – even when it came to their food. Fancy interrupted Sasha's trance.

"Sasha, I think you're just greedy. You know doggone well Ms. Tootsie's food is delicious and Philly's finest. And dang, girl. Slow down. The plate's not going anywhere."

Sasha looked embarrassed and took a quick break from her food.

"I know. I'm so used to speed eating at work I can't help but to eat fast. I hate having 20-minute breaks and 12 minutes to eat that nasty ass food." Then Sasha's expression changed and she leaned over and said, "I'm ready to hear your story."

"So that's the whole story huh, Fancy?" Sasha questioned her. The two ladies paid their bill and tipped the waitress very well. Sasha even went back to drop $10 more on the table because she knew how it was to work for tips. On the walk to their cars Sasha reiterated what Fancy had told her.

"Let me get this straight. You were creeping with Tamal that whole last year before we graduated, and you used Tashad's mistake as an excuse to go to the prom with Tamal as friends so I wouldn't figure you two out. Then you found out you were pregnant so you decided to bounce with Tamal to Philly and next you two dummies met a chick named after a damned car walking out of the doctor's office. You two dummies gambled and took her up on an offer you *thought* you couldn't refuse. In the meantime you two dummies bounced over the bridge and the car lady got both of you dummies a job. Since you were pregnant you took an office job as an assistant attorney's secretary, which I'm not even sure is a real job title. Tamal started working as a dealer at Legacy. Unfortunately you two dummies moved into a townhome in Tamal's name only. *How smart was he?* Then you found out he had a bad drinking problem, so dummy number one listened to the damned car lady again and left dummy number two to move into your own crib in Chester."

Sasha raised an eyebrow waiting on Fancy to butt in. "Is that correct?" Fancy felt embarrassed as they both walked to their cars. She knew it sounded weird to Sasha and Sasha would never have understood unless she walked in her shoes. Fancy nodded in agreement. "You got it, cousin."

"Sasha, it's not what it seems like. Corvette is a nice lady and she just wanted to help us out that's all," Fancy said. "Yes, I played a dummy for a couple of years thinking Tamal was going to get himself together again. Everything was going fine in the beginning, but once he started complaining about Legacy he started changing so I had to take Baby Tamal away from him. My son doesn't need to be in a negative environment, especially heavy drinking. Sasha, if it's all right with you we can have family day next week so you can meet your little cousin Tamal in person?"

"Sounds good to me cousin, by the way I'm sorry for calling you a dummy."

"It's okay. I did make some dumb decisions in my time, but like Angela Bassett Fancy got her groove back." Fancy smiled as she buckled her seatbelt and drove off feeling comfortable in her own skin.

Once Sasha saw Baby Tamal she knew he wasn't Tamal's son. *Now why the hell did dummy number two think he got dummy number one pregnant? If Tamal can't see that baby Tamal is Tashad Trader's son he really does have a drinking problem.*

"Oh my, look at his gorgeous eyes." That's the first thing Sasha noticed because they were the same green eyes Fancy fell in love with years ago-otherwise Tashad Trader.

"Yes, he has big eyes just like Tamal," Fancy proclaimed. Sasha wanted to tell Fancy so bad to get a grip because she reminded her of women who wanted their children to look like their fathers when either they looked like their *real* daddy or just like the mother. Now, sadly, her cousin was one of those crazy women. Sasha played tug-of-war in her mind as she watched Baby Tamal run around The Philadelphia Zoo. Her inner soul wanted to scream -- *Tamal Jackson, you are NOT THE FATHER* – but she couldn't do it. *Where is Maury when you need him,* she sighed to herself.

Chapter 16

BREAK-ROOM

"Hey, Tamal!"

"Braze, what are you so happy about? Oh, you must have seen your sweetheart already." Braze's smile was bigger than the Joker's. She had just gotten a quickie in the women's bathroom. She was a big girl, but Braze always felt big girls needed love, too.

"No, I haven't bumped into my boss yet but a player just tipped us $5,000," Braze said telling a bald-faced lie.

"That's great Braze," Tamal said, "because the players at my table suck. They're all as young as shit and whine every time they lose a hand. They beg me to break, but they don't want to tip. I'm ready to take all their money in Blackjack, but the cards keep going in their favor."

Braze continued making her coffee and turned toward Sasha who was standing on her left.

"This girl had some funky *MB's* on, Sash," Braze said.

"What's that?" Tamal asked.

"*OMG.* That's a new clothing line. I just bought her pocketbook, *My Bagg*. The big print makes the bag look hot. It cost me two paychecks."

Tamal stood up. "You spent *two checks* on a pocketbook that says *My Bagg*," Tamal said incredulously. "Are you crazy? Don't even answer because you are."

"Tamal you don't need to talk. You spend your two days off drinking vodka, vodka and more vodka. You're probably as broke as hell now. I'd rather buy clothes and pocketbooks, something tangible I can wear and use, than gulp down my check like you do."

"Calm down you two," Braze jumped in between them. "Look at the rest of the dealers looking at us. I don't even know why they keep scheduling all of us on the same breaks. I'm not looking forward to four more breaks with you two today."

"You're right" Tamal acknowledged. The dealers marched back to the gaming floor, and they all heard loud screams from pit area 21. Braze, Tamal and Sasha walked in the opposite direction from the drama. "Security, Security," Pitt Boss Jerry shouted from the top of his lungs. A tall black man with salt and pepper hair was pointing his finger in Dealer Trox's face. Trox was a short Asian dealer that never said a word to anyone. His back was facing Sasha, Braze, and Tamal as they continued walking to their table, so they really couldn't see what was going on. All they heard was the black man shouting that he didn't want a hit and for the bosses to review the tapes.

"Wow, what the heck is going on? Trox never bothers anybody," Braze thought as she tapped on her table. Nearby, Tamal and Sasha were wondering the exact same thing.

"Man, Trox has made somebody mad," Tamal said as he tapped on his table. "Yo, J.T. Go find out the real deal," Tamal demanded. J.T. said good luck to his players as he cleared his hands and tapped off. "Man, I'm not wasting my break for you," J.T. said and walked away from Pit Area 10.

I wish a player would put his finger in my face like he's doing Trox, I'd just have to lose my job because I would knock the shit out of him or her. Just like on 'Trapped Dealers' Nina wasn't having it. She took the card dispenser and knocked the mess out of the player who tried to throw a drink on her. Sasha's mind was always reliving "Trapped Dealers" episodes. Eventually she realized they were all trapped dealers at Legacy. After a few more breaks and debates on various topics Sasha got into a debate with an animal lover, Bob, about Michael Vick.

"Yea, I know he was wrong but he paid his price for it," Sasha defended Vick. "That's more than I can say about the Casey Anthony case. Of course I realize she was acquitted by a jury, and only God knows who killed her baby, Sasha said. Yet they bashed Michael Vick over a dog. Man, this world is so twisted." Braze had to hold Sasha back from Bob, who wasn't feeling Sasha talking about dogs.

"Sasha, he was wrong and he should have gotten more time," Bob shouted.

I wish Leona was here, Sasha thought. *Who are we to judge Michael Vick or Casey Anthony? We all have a price to pay to The Man Above.* Now Sasha was yelling over Braze's shoulder as she tried to loosen from her tight bear hug. "Braze, thank God you held me," Sasha said while straightening her uniform. "Girrrrl, Bob's not worth it – smelling like those stinking dogs of his," Braze said covering her nose. Both ladies chuckled as they exited the break room.

At the end of the night the dealers raced out of Legacy like they were running the 100-meter dash. It's so funny how more people say goodbye when leaving work than hello when coming to work. Legacy was such a miserable place to work 'til people felt almost like they were being released from jail when they get off – thus the extreme jubilation.

Sasha, Braze, Tamal and Leona always waited for each other and walked to their cars together. Tonight there were only three of them because Leona was on vacation. They were all exhausted but enjoying the 80-degree weather.

"Wow, look at the moon," Sasha pointed.

"That's why all of those players were acting a fool tonight," Tamal said.

"Mally they act like a fool every damned night," Sasha countered.

"Yup. They sure do. We just have to know how to keep our composure because we already know what we're getting ourselves into when we clock in," Braze said. Before unlocking their cars all three greeted each other with hugs and said goodnight.

"Goodnight guys. I'll see you all tomorrow. I forgot something," Braze said as she swiftly ran back into Legacy.

"Mally, you know what she forgot, right? She definitely has some issues." Sasha said.

"I know what she forgot, but that's on her. If she wants to play, let her be, Sash," Tamal said while waving goodbye to Sasha. Then he turned up his music and grooved to Michael Jackson all the way home.

Chapter 17

LEONA

"Goooood morning, baby," Lamont said with excitement. He kissed his wife Leona on the cheek knowing today was the first day of her much-needed and much-deserved two-week vacation. "I know you're happy to be out of that hell hole for a minute," Lamont said. As he spoke, he wondered why Leona didn't appear happier about being off.

"Its morning already honey?" she asked while fumbling with her jet black curly hair. "Yes it is, Honey." Lamont looked at his wife with sadness because he knew he was doing her so wrong. If only she could understand he needed a freak in the sheets instead of a pure and holy woman. *Besides, we're married so why in world is she acting like we're dating,* he thought. In the beginning of their relationship Lamont couldn't keep Leona off of him. She was a bigger freak than your average porn chick, but something happened in the midst of their years when she rededicated her life to The Lord. Lamont felt as though Leona left him to be with Jesus. Little did Mr. Romeo know Jesus had revealed to her that Lamont was really a big 'ole sex freak.

Leona started babbling about how she had to get up and cook breakfast for the children, whom she did right by no matter what. "I have to pack extra snacks because Monty has practice today," she said. "By the way, don't forget to pick him up after practice. You know how you get sidetracked at the office." Leona gave Lamont a twisted look as if she knew what really had been going down at Frisby and Trappe Law firm. Lamont ignored her expression. He never wanted to battle with her thoughts or opinions because he knew sooner or later she and Jesus would tag team him. And when Jesus came to her rescue he knew it took days to put her out – just like a raging forest fire. No matter how much backup Lamont had, Holy Ghost watered him down every time. So instead, he just listened to and agreed with his lovely wife.

"Ahh…Ohhh." Leona had her head in her hands, wondering how she was going to cook the children's breakfast with the awful headache she had. "What's wrong, honey," Lamont asked, fearing she'd caught another one of her bad headaches. It seemed like two to three times a week after she pulled eight hours at Legacy Leona awakened with a horrible headache. At first Lamont thought she used that as an excuse not to make crazy love to him like she used to, but when her doctor diagnosed she suffered from stress-induced migraines he realized she wasn't faking just to get out of making love. Lamont insisted on caring for the children so she could get some proper rest.

"I'll make sure the children have what they need. You lie back down and get some rest hon," said Lamont, whose love outweighed his faults in Leona's book any given day. He went into the bathroom, reached for a Dixie cup, poured Leona some water and gave her two Advil's. He didn't know she had taken two Advil's just minutes before while he was in the shower.

"Here, baby. Take this. I feel your pain." Lamont tried to sympathize with her aches. Leona rose from their plush Pillow Top bed and popped the pills in her mouth, thinking it probably couldn't do any harm to take a few more. *So what if I just popped two? Maybe this headache will go away sooner* she thought while quickly gulping down the pills. Then she lay back down and put the pillow over her face. If Lamont didn't know better he would have thought she was suffocating herself. *Female issues,* he thought while continuing to dress for work. Lamont commended Leona for being a great mom. He knew she wasn't like most moms who constantly complained about how bad their children were and couldn't wait to send them off to school so they could have peace in the house.

If women practiced more abstinence or waited until marriage versus just settling for any man they'd be much better off. Women need men who will be there through thick and thin, men who are ready to support their families under any circumstances. When men step up to the plate, usually their children grow up with better outlooks on life.

Leona moved the pillow from her face to see why Lamont was making such a terrible sound. *And they say I can't sing. Hmmm. He's really trying to carry a note.* Leona wondered why Lamont was so happy this morning but felt in due time God would reveal his sneakiness to her.

"Honey, can you lower your voice? My head is pounding, and it feels like I'm being hit with a hammer," Leona said while wondering what was up with the unnecessary tunes.

Lamont leaned over and gave her a peck on her soft, juicy lips.

"Babe, I just felt like humming a tune. I'm sorry if I startled you," Lamont lied.

Leona got up and put on her pink and red heart-shaped robe with matching slippers that she purchased from a flea market to help support breast cancer awareness. Lamont asked where she was going because he could have sworn she just said her head was pounding terribly.

"I'm going to check on the children if you don't mind, Babyface."

"Ahhh shux. What have I done to be called Babyface?" he asked, smiling from ear to ear. Leona used to call him Babyface all of the time just before she made ridiculous love to him. *Oh how I remember it all so well. The first time she called me Babyface she said from now on, Lamont, you're mine, Babyface.*

Dang, Leona, those were the days when we used to make crazy love. Well, those days are over, I guess. Still, Lamont wondered whether Leona was hinting at pending intimacy until she burst his bubble.

"What were you just singing, Whip Appeal by Babyface right?" Leona asked. "Damn, Leona. You sure know how to soften my manhood." Leona giggled. "Sorry, Ba—I mean Lamont." She giggled again. Even though her headache was getting worse, she just wanted to say good morning and give the kids a hug before they headed off to school.

Like a concerned parent, Leona knew there was no guarantee the kids would return home, so she made it her duty to make them feel loved every chance she got. Leona stepped into the hallway and looked over her shining marble Cherry banister. It was the first time in months she could remember the children getting along. Usually she had to scream like a mad woman to get them to keep their voices down in the morning. Kiya, 15, was the oldest. She sported a short bob haircut and was the spitting image of her estranged father. She was a little tall for her age and had a small frame. She had honey brown skin with a few freckles on her cheeks. Lamont was not her biological father; however, he took care of her as if he was.

Leona and Lamont began dating when Kiya was 2. She was very intelligent and loved playing mommy, especially when her parents weren't around.

Then there was 12-year-old Monty. He was a starting quarterback for his school, and although he was a little shorter than Kiya he was ready to tackle her every chance he got.

Last but not least there was smart and witty Lynae, 10. She was always full of questions and hated when her parents left Kiya in charge.

Leona smiled at the children, who didn't notice her. She decided not to bother them this morning. Lamont had already said he would ensure they got what they needed, and she figured their hugs, especially if too tight, could exacerbate her headache. She turned and walked back to her bedroom. In seconds she was in her comfortable Pillow Top bed once again.

Lamont informed Leona he would tell the children to allow her to rest when they got home from school. He would explain to them why she didn't come downstairs this morning like she always did. The older two children would understand, but he knew his little one, a lawyer in the making, would have him on the witness stand about her mother.

Lamont had on a pink shirt, dark blue slacks, a blue blended tie and a tailor-made jacket. He had a feeling Corvette would like his new look today. It was very different form the plain old black and white suits he often wore. Leona could feel in her body that today would be different from any other day. She grabbed the bottle of Advil from the nightstand and took two more. *Headache, please go away soon.*

"You're looking sharp. What's the special occasion? I don't recall you saying you had court. First you were singing and now you're dressed to cheat," Leona said.

"*Dressed to cheat.* How do you do that?" Lamont asked. He brushed his hair and sprayed some Calvin Klein cologne. He wondered how her intuition could be right on point and started feeling like he was married to Bewitched. "Babes, I just feel like dressing nice like the weather," he lied. Lamont waited a minute in the bathroom to hear a response from her so she wouldn't see his expression – a dead giveaway that he was lying.

A woman knows when her man is cheating even if she wants to be in denial. And women should stop letting men run game on them.

Man, snap out of it. Corvette is no good for you. Lamont's conscious was speaking to him… After realizing he never heard a response he assumed the coast was clear. So he took a final look at his waves in the mirror then walked back into the bedroom and noticed his sleeping beauty was out cold. *Ah. Thank God for Advil.* Now Leona couldn't give him the third degree since she was in fairytale land. He stroked the side of her face three times and gave her a peck on the cheek before whispering "I love you."

Lamont reached for his briefcase then turned the house phone and Leona's cell phone off. He knew she needed to get some restful sleep and didn't want to risk Sasha, Tamal or Braze calling with all of their troubles and issues or for advice from her. What she dealt with at work was dreadful enough. She didn't need to be bothered on her vacation with stories about the on-goings at Legacy. The less she heard about that place right now, the better.

"Good morning, my super children. Daddy's here to save the day and will be sending you all off to school," Lamont said.

"Where's mommy," Lynae yelled, her two pigtails flying in the air as she jumped up and down in the kitchen.

"Dad, you know you have to pick me up from practice today," Monty said. Lamont wasn't surprised Monty spoke with such authority. The last couple of times he was supposed to pick him up he was late because he was fooling around with his mistress, and his coach had to bring him home. You'd think that taught him to pick up his son on time, but Lamont still wanted to play in the sandbox.

"Yea son. I know. I'll be there. Just make sure you make at least one touchdown," Lamont said. Monty ran through the oversized family room holding his football in his right hand. He threw the ball down and screamed TOUCHDOWN!

"See dad. Already done."

"I see." *I meant on the field not in my house* Lamont thought.

"So dad, does this mean I have to keep an eye on Lynae?" Kiya asked. Lynae rudely interrupted.

"No...no...nooooo...daddy. I don't want Kiya babysitting me. She always thinks she's my boss."

"If your mother is still resting, yes, Kiya will have to keep an eye on you. Your mother is still in the house so Kiya is not the boss over you." Lamont made things very clear to the girls as he packed their lunches.

"Ok, daddy. Just hurry up home puleeze," Lynae whined.

"Little girl, I'm the boss of you," Kiya said just to mess with Lynae.

"No you're not, Kiya. See daddy. I told you."

"Girls, cut it out. Nobody's the boss except your mom and I, now get ready for the bus. I don't have time to drop you off if you miss it." Lamont hugged the girls and gave his son a manly handshake.

"You got it dad," Monty said.

"Ok daddy," said Kiya.

"Bye dad. I loooooove yoooou," Lynae sang. Lamont waved at them as they ran for the bus. He turned off the phone in the kitchen and the other one in the hallway where all of the family pictures hung.

Why do I keep doing the things I'm doing. I know I love my wife, but on the other hand I love how Corvette makes me feel. Lamont still remembered the first day Corvette came for the interview. After taking one look at her double D's he felt forced to hire her. He had to hire her, but he had no intention of having sex with her. He fantasized about having sex with her and prayed a time would come when he stopped thinking only about sex.

Chapter 18

TAMAL

"A-yo. How many pounds are you benching?" asked the attractive man who appeared to be in his mid 20s. Tamal answered with confidence since he knew he was a couple of years older and a few pounds heavier than him.

"I'm benching 80 young buck. What do you know 'bout that?"

"Well come over here and spot me then tell me what ya think," the young man said. Before Tamal stood in front of the bench he noticed an older woman with a tight shape glide past him. *Damn! I bet old head had it going on back in the day.*

The young man gave Tamal the chrome bar to hold with 60 pounds on each side.

"Hold this for a minute," young buck said before positioning himself on the bench.

"Ahhhh. Get this shit young'in," Tamal said in an exasperated tone. "Yo old head. My bad. I thought you could handle a young buck like me," he said sarcastically. "By the way," I'm benching 120 easily to answer your question." Young buck chuckled and proceeded to take the bar from Tamal's arms.

"Thanks." *I've got to stop drinking. I'm losing my strength,"* Tamal whispered under his breath, hoping young buck didn't hear him.

"Sure. Blame it on the liquor," young buck said while wiping sweat off his six pack and muscular honey-toned biceps. "See ya around old head."

Tamal had never been so embarrassed in his life, other than the time Sasha played make-up lady on his face. How could he not feel that red lipstick caked on his face and those extra eyelashes? That's the day he swore he would never sleep on her mother's couch again. Tamal massaged his sore arms and walked out of the gym with thoughts of renewing his membership at Gym Land.

You have three new voice mail messages and one saved message. To listen to your new voice messages press one. *"Hey Tamal this is Sadie. I really enjoyed our date last night. Give me a call when you get this message.* To save this message, hit 1. Tamal hit 7 to erase Sadie's message. *"Hi, T."* Tamal next heard the sweet sound of Fancy's voice and jumped right up off the couch and pointed the remote toward his 56" flat screen TV. He needed complete silence while listening to Fancy's voice. He knew she would eventually come around and figured it had been too long since he'd seen his son, Baby T. *"It's been a while now and Baby Tamal is getting older. He's playing football and baseball now so I want you to be a part of his life. Call me at my new number when you get a chance."* Tamal knew he had missed a few years already, but knew for a fact Fancy hadn't missed any of those child support checks. Tamal was trying to figure out why she was surfacing at this time. *Why does Fancy want me to "play daddy" now,* he thought. Message three: *"Hey, Mally. Yo the job was crazy packed today. Call me back sucker. By the way, I know all about you and my cuz. Man up daddy.* Tamal realized Sasha and Fancy had engaged in a girl's chat. *I bectha the bitch told only her side of the story.* Tamal figured two could play that game, so he returned Sasha's call first.

"Yo Sash. I see you spoke with my baby's mom, huh?"

"Yea, we had a long talk. As a matter fact we ate lunch at Ms. Tootsie's after she asked Mrs. Greenwire about babysitting Baby Tamal." *Oh that's why the wench wants me to start getting Tamal. She needs a babysitter. Shame on her,* Tamal thought with disgust.

"Yea, Tamal. Fancy just wanted what's best for the kid. He didn't need to see you drunk like that," Sasha said, making it clear she knew Tamal had trouble with the bottle.

"Sometimes I feel like he isn't my son," Tamal said, expressing doubts about paternity. Bingo, fellas. If you feel you might be loving, nurturing and financially supporting a child that isn't yours, make it your business to get a blood test ASAP.

"Hmmm." Sasha changed the subject quicker than a person could drown in quicksand. "Man, you should have been at work. Believe me when I tell you the freaks came out at the Legacy tonight. There was this white chick passing through with a half-ass leather jacket on with no clothes underneath. All of her trash was hanging out and those hungry growling co-workers of ours couldn't watch their games to save their erupted manhood.

"Ah Sash come now," Tamal said with excitement, wanting to hear more. "Like what kind of trash did she have hanging out?"Tamal could only imagine. A month prior when he met Sadie she had all of her trash hanging out. For Tamal it was eye candy. Sadie was wearing a pair of black pants that looked like they were painted on. Tamal didn't want to get tangled up with Sadie because she scared him half to death once she got undressed. *Damn, mama. It looks like you just jumped out of a crayon box with all of those tattoos on your body.* Despite what he was thinking, Tamal handled his business like a man that night and gave Sadie back shots. That's when he noticed she used her tush for a chalkboard, too. *This broad got too many tats and pierces for me.* Tamal felt relieved when he left Sadie's place.

"Oh, I forgot you're one of them who can't keep his head in his pants," Sasha said. "All of you men who lust will get what you're asking for. By the way, your mom said she loves you. My break is up. See ya." Tamal knew it was time to pay his mom a visit even though she had been keeping the family secret of her own daughter being molested for all of these years.

On the real, women. There's nothing that should keep you from protecting your children. Tell authorities if your children are being molested – no matter who the perpetrator is – and get your children some counseling to deal with the abuse. Do whatever you have to, by any means necessary, to protect your children from sexual predators.

Chapter 19

TAMAL

"**C**oming out, craps 11 any seven. Tamal pushed the dice out to the next player on the right side of him.

"Give me the dice the way they land," the gray haired black man yelled. Tamal pushed the dice in front of him.

"Are you going to shoot?" Tamal asked.

"Not until you say you're going to give them to me the way they land." *This player is just being a complete fool thinking I supposed to bow down to him,* Tamal thought. Fortunately a supervisor stepped in to address the matter.

"Sir, my dealer heard you. You got it. Exactly the way they land they'll be returned back to you." Tamal shook his head in disgust at the supervisor's kowtowing to the player.

"Thanks, George," the shooter shouted before picking up the dice and throwing them down the other end of the dice table.

"SEVEN OUT," Tamal screamed. "Next shooter. Next." *Out of here, old man.*

"asshole," the old man yelled at Tamal. "All because of this dealer I lost my freaking money. Get him off the game."

"Sir, there's no need to speak like that about my dealer," George said. "Tamal did just as you wanted him to do. He gave you the dice the way they landed."

"Yea, but his attitude sucks. I'll be writing this casino about your awful dealer," he mumbled while walking away from the table.

Now they see why I drink after work. These players are all shot the hell out, Tamal thought as his mind wandered while he placed the dice to the next player.

"Would you like a hard four, ma'm?" Tamal asked since the point she threw was four. "No, just give me the dice," the woman replied. "If I wanted a hard four I would have asked for one. Hurry and give me the damn dice." *Man, today isn't my day. The point is four bitch. I'm just doing my job. Hurry up 4 a.m. so I can get out of the heck out of this hell hole.* Tamal felt his time to clock out couldn't come fast enough.

After Tamal's long night at work he eased up to his doorstep and turned the key in the lock. He went straight to his bedroom to grab his best friend, vodka, while taking off his smoke-filled uniform. *This is for the players,* he thought before taking a quick shot to the head. Then he pressed play on the DVD to watch his favorite movie, "All About the Benjamins." Between scenes he gulped down a second shot. *Now this one is for the co-workers. What a pain in the ass they can be.*

Tamal picked up a cracker and spit it out almost as soon as he bit into it because he'd left the package open causing the crackers to turn stale. He pressed the message button on his answering machine while falling into the comfort of his 800 thread count sheets on his king-sized bed. He lay back as the messages started playing.

BEEP: "Tamal, this is Fancy. Why in the hell did you tell Baby Tamal you were coming to his baseball game if you weren't coming? You knew he was looking forward to you being there." Tamal smacked himself upside the head for forgetting all about his little man's game. He felt bad and promised himself he would make it up to him.

Beep: "Hey son, this is your mother. I hope all's well. I haven't spoken to you since I called about your father. Tamal, your father's dead now. Return my call baby boy. I love you." Naydine stressed the word love. Tamal knew his life was changing now that he and Fancy were trying to get on the right track for Baby Tamal's sake. For a while he just couldn't seem to bring himself to get into the fatherhood role given he never had love for his father. He kept trying to figure out whether his father had dampened his ability to reason as a man or whether the alcohol was getting the best of him. He laid his head back against his pillow and listened to the last message.

Beep: "Hey there, daddy. I haven't seen you since we last went out. I hope I didn't turn you off. You have to excuse me, but I haven't had sex in over a year and you were looking so good in your ROC sweat suit I just had to give it up. Please call me back, daddy."

Stop lying, bitch, Tamal said out loud. "My man J.T. told me he smashed that tush a week before I did." Tamal enjoyed living a bachelor's life. He didn't have to answer to anyone and figured he could wine and dine whomever he wanted. Now that Fancy was out of the picture Tamal wanted someone like Jade, who he initially considered wife material. Yet after J.T. told him how much of a ho Jade was he knew she wouldn't become Mrs. Tamal Jackson. Jade looked as good as Ms. Corvette with a perfect ass, perfect lips and perfect hips. I could have Jade as my wife easily. *Damn shame she shared her fruit with my main man.*

The next morning Tamal had an awful hangover. The sun shone so brightly through his room you would have thought it rose right there at the foot of his bed. He was so busy entertaining himself with vodka shots the night before he had forgotten to close his curtains. We all know once you start drinking your mind goes in different directions. Tamal turned over and looked at the clock that was connected to his answering machine, which had flashing messages.

Aw, man it's almost 2 o'clock in the afternoon. He raced to his cell to see if he could catch J.T. because they were supposed to have gone to the gym at 1 p.m. Of course he got no answer. J.T. was probably getting his work out on with young buck by now. Thanks to his vodka Tamal had missed out again. He realized he still had time to drive over to Chester to meet his little man before school recessed at 3:15 p.m.

Fancy and Tamal had agreed he could start picking their son up after school on his days off, so they could get reconnected. Tamal wanted to do everything in his power to build a better relationship with his son. He knew it was too late to rekindle a friendship with his father, but as for Baby Tamal he wanted to start a relationship with him. Tamal reached over and pressed play.

Beep: "Tamal. This is your mother, Going to the ------. Naydine's voice sounded desperate and dry.

Tamal jumped up and dialed his mother's house. No answer. Next he ran to his cell and turned it on so he could retrieve the numbers of his sister, Kymbah, and his halfbrother, Kevin, Jr.

Kevin, Jr. was another one of Mr. Jackson's mistakes from his past. Tamal never held it against Kevin, Jr. for just popping up on their doorstep and never departing.

"Honey, I know I lied about cheating on you. I'm sorry. The ho didn't get an abortion even though that's what she told me she was using the money for. Well, now Kevin Jackson, Jr. is sitting in our living room with no place to go," Tamal remembered hearing his father tell his mother.

"Kevin, I have forgiven you one too many times. How can you keep on hurting me like this?" Naydine cried.

As Tamal continued replaying that conversation in his mind, he remembered his father apologizing while he hugged his mom as tightly as he could.

"The boy is 12 now and his mom wants to bring him in my life, for us to get to know each other." He went on to say Kevin, Jr.'s mother was unfit and had just gotten caught in a drug bust.

"You better be thankful I'm a better woman than most," Naydine said with obvious anger and hurt in her voice. *"But I tell you what, Kevin. You'll be the one responsible for Kevin, Jr. You'll clean up after him and where you go, he'll go, too. I'm not a babysitter or Benson, but he is welcomed to live here."*

Tamal learned to love Kevin, Jr. – from a distance. He knew he planned to cross the bridge as soon as he graduated.

All kind of bizarre thoughts raced through Tamal's head about his mother. *Was she okay? Did she pass out?* He dialed his sister's and half-brother's cells once again. Still no answer. Now Tamal was beginning to panic. *Why wasn't anybody picking up their phone? WTF.* Tamal changed his plans from driving to Chester to see his son to dashing to Camden to see about his mother. He grabbed his Gucci shades, threw on his khaki Capri's and tank T-shirt. He was getting used to flexing his muscles now that young buck was training him at the gym.

He waved to Mrs. Greenwire as she played in her flower garden. She waved back. Tamal raced off and Mrs. Greenwire shook her head. *Be careful, Nascar.* Tamal's music was pumping so loud he never heard his cell phone ring or vibrate the whole ride to Camden. Tamal made the drive in a hop, skip and a jump. At one point J.T. blew the horn at him to say hi, but Tamal's music was playing so loudly he didn't even notice his friend passing him over the Ben Franklin Bridge. *I'm talking to the man in the mirror. I'm asking him to change his ways.* Tamal sang along to one of the late Michael Jackson's biggest hits. It took only a few seconds for him to realize he was giving himself some much-needed advice, not just singing along to M.J.

Right before Tamal crossed the bridge into Camden on Haddon Avenue he passed an accident, which he figured was the cause of the traffic jam he encountered prior to reaching Camden. He noticed he had two missed calls, one from Fancy and the other from his mother's cell phone. He pressed redial to listen.

"Tamal, now I tried to give you chance after chance and you kept disappointing me. This is it! DO NOT CALL US ANYMORE."

"Shut the hell up, bitch," Tamal yelled at the phone. "I was on my way to see Baby Tamal but something important came up!" Tamal wanted to call Fancy to explain that he really wanted to spend time with his son today, but instead he redialed his mother's number. The lady who answered spoke with so much pain in her voice Tamal could tell she had been crying. After she got herself together she began speaking with attitude.

"It's about time you called back. We've been trying to contact you all morning," she sobbed.

"Put mom on the phone. She called me in the middle of the night crying and it sounded like she couldn't breathe," Tamal angrily snapped back. *Why in the heck did Kymbah answer mom's cell phone anyway? Where was mom?* Tamal's panic and the uneasy feeling in his gut were increasing rapidly. "Put her on the phone...is she all right? Where is she?"

It was evident Tamal was really worried at this point.

Before he could throw another question Kymbah's way she spoke again.

"No, she isn't all right," Kymbah said through sobs. "Tamal she died at 9:45 a.m. this morning."

Chapter 20

LEONA

L amont took one last look at the bright orange and
yellow kitchen he'd promised to repaint on weekends
but never did. He locked up the house and set out the
garbage before hopping in his deep sea blue metallic BMW
128. He turned on his radio to hear "Brick House" by The
Commodores. Lamont drove through Center City singing one
of his all-time favorite songs. *She's a brick house. She's mighty,
mighty, just letting it all hang out.* As he sang, he thought about
Samantha Mellon. *Wow, I would like to see how she looks now. She
was definitely a brick house back in the day. Oh, how those were the
good 'ole days.* Then a negative thought crossed his mind. *What
if she had six to eight kids and is now grossly overweight?* Lamont
shook Samantha Mellon out of his mind quickly as he pulled
up into his Law firm on Market Street. He proceeded to park
and heard a streaky loud voice coming from behind as one of
his clients walked toward him in distress.

"Mr. Trappe." Lamont turned around, took one look and
knew what she wanted.

"Good morning, Mrs. Smith."

"Yea, yea," she said, ignoring his greeting. "Cut the crap.
I'll get straight to the point. I need to know how fast you can
get this divorce over with and find out where my money is.
I've been waiting out here over half an hour for you to pull
up."

Mrs. Smith had her hand on her hips waiting for Lamont to say something stupid.

"Mrs., I mean Ms. Smith, I'm not scheduled to be in my office until 9 a.m., and if I'm reading my watch correctly it's five minutes 'til 9 and your appointment isn't until later this morning."

Lamont glanced twice at his watch hoping she got the hint to come back at her appointed time.

"Well, I know all of that. I just wanted to let you know I found out some more dirt on my husband, my soon-to-be ex-husband," she said with attitude. "Okay. I'll see you in my office. Just give me a few minutes then you can come up," Lamont said with a look of confusion.

"I'm going to have breakfast at the Hard Rock Café. Would you like anything Mr. Trappe?" She adjusted her MB pocket-book over her shoulder.

"No, I'm fine Ms. Smith. See you in a few," Lamont said while walking to the elevators.

Lamont replayed Mrs. Lisa Smith's case back and forth in his head, yet couldn't remember it at all. He knew she was a wife who was out to suck her husband dry. That was one thing Lisa and Leona had in common. If his wife ever found out he was cheating, she would suck his well dry, too. What a bad predicament to be in. Lamont knew he had to cut Corvette off soon and prayed he would never have to walk in Mr. Smith's shoes.

Lamont had been planning to stop his affair with Corvette. He just felt like Leona wasn't giving him any attention in the bedroom. She always acted like Jesus was standing over them watching, so she never completely released her body to him anymore. Once he met Corvette and she was willing to be his daytime freak without any strings attached Lamont couldn't resist. He became blind to the fact he still had a wife and children at home, but his fantasy would soon catch up with his reality. In due time.

Corvette Ford and Leona Trappe were very attractive but very opposite from each other. One woman loved God with all of her heart; the other woman called on God only when having an orgasm. They both had curves that made you want to lose weight. Corvette brought life to Lamont versus Leona who spoke life over him. Even though he knew his wife meant well, sometimes he wished she would get buck wild like she did in the good 'ole days and turn into the freak he had been missing. Besides using Legacy or headaches as an excuse, all she did was complain about how much quiet time she needed.

Corvette Ford was a great secretary and had been doing her job for three years. She became so good that two other lawyers wanted her to work exclusively for them, prompting her to find an assistant secretary to help out with all of the work she had accumulated. At the time Fancy was a great candidate. Corvette never met her boss' wife, Leona, and often wondered why she never stopped by the office to bring him lunch or anything. *As fine as Mr. Trappe is, who wouldn't want to lick the Hershey chocolate off his nuts,* Corvette thought.

Corvette had seen only a picture of Leona. Lamont had one photo of her holding the Bible that sat on his desk. Every time Corvette walked in he tried to subtly lay it down, but sometimes Corvette got close enough to kiss Leona through the picture frame.

Oh how often Corvette wished pictures could see. There would be so many people hurt, lost, devastated and even divorced. Corvette was the lonely secretary who fulfilled other women's husbands' dreams with her double D's and the quickies she loved giving – especially to Lamont every chance she got.

Leona had it going on, and Lamont would be a fool to throw away their relationship over some office fling. His wife had her own job, money and, of course they had three adorable kids that he loved dearly. And Leona was a brick house despite delivering three children naturally. But in Lamont's eyes she lost her sex appeal as she got deeper into Christ. So given Corvette was always in freak mode, Lamont didn't see anything wrong with having both women. He often fantasized about having them together, though he knew Leona would never go for that. He knew in his heart sooner or later he had to let Corvette go. She did great work for him and made him feel oh, so good, but he still knew it had to end. His mindset was like that of any other cheating man. He didn't think of it as cheating as long as he didn't get caught. And if he got caught he already had a lie mapped out. *Oh honey this was my first time, and I swear it will never happen again.* Lamont felt he had invested too much time and money to give it all up for Corvette. Yet, on the other hand, Corvette made him happy and in some pathetic ways he needed her.

Chapter 21

LEONA

"**G**ood morning Mister." Corvette was wearing the flirtiest expression on her face, making Lamont want to jump on her with quickness. "You're looking mighty sexy this morning."

"Ah…you know business as usual," Lamont slurred while fumbling with his tie, as if it wasn't already as straight as a number two pencil. He tried his hardest to avoid looking at Corvette's double D's; however, like most men he couldn't help himself, especially given he had already had many slices of her pie.

"Mister, you know I'm horny. I didn't see you all last week because you've been on these so-called important business meetings," Corvette said sarcastically as if she was his wife.

The nerve of Corvette – and others like her – to question a married man. Women who chose to sleep with married men usually got what they deserved, but Corvette didn't see it that way. Of course, if she kept playing with fire sooner or later she would get burned, especially considering the man she was fooling around with was the husband of a child of God. "I hope you're not doing a triple on me," Corvette said. "A triple! What's that?" Lamont asked as he entered his spacious office that was nearly the size of a three-car garage. The office had very little furniture, with a cushioned bench on the left side and file cabinets and two antique Mahogany chairs on the right side. Leona had picked up the chairs for him at a flea market.

"Are you doing a third woman? I'm already your double," Corvette said with a wry smile.

"Naw...naw...naw. I've just been tied up on some business accounts. *Hell, I'm not even doing my first woman*, Lamont thought.

"Ok Missssster. Let's cut to the chase. When are you going to tell your wife? Better yet--- when are you going to leave her ass?" Corvette demanded an answer right then and there. Her left leg was hiked on his desk, exposing all of her pudding underneath a red puffed skirt.

"Now girl you," Lamont started to speak but couldn't help but glance under her skirt and notice her goodies. Damn, she never did this before, he thought. "No, I'm not ready to leave my wife. And why aren't you wearing any panties today?" he asked, partly in shock. "You, we both agreed not to catch feelings anyhow. So where's all of this talk about me leaving my wife and stuff coming from?" Lamont's erect manhood was thinking for him now that he'd seen her clean, shapely shaven garden. All he could think was *one last time, one last time. Then I'll tell her it's over.*

Men really think it's that easy, but it's not.

He couldn't resist her Dolce & Gabbana; the aroma was driving him insane. He began stuttering "C---orrrrvette, we both agreed we wouldn't we wouldn't catch feelings over our sex-capades." He was hoping she heard him the second time around about not developing feelings. Instead, she ignored him as she plopped her foot down on the floor and proceeded to step closer to him.

"First of all, Mister, I'm tired of playing your board games. I'm ready to be the star of the game," Corvette boasted. "Secondly, I never agreed to that feelings bullshit. That was you doing all of the talking. Third, I'm wearing no panties to spice things up in the office. It's called easy access."

Oh my, she's starting to frighten me. What the hell was I thinking? Lamont knew he had to put a stop to this affair with quickness.

"Come on mister. I know you want it," Corvette teased. As bad as Lamont wanted to throw her up against his waxed maple wood desk and suck her breasts until they were soggy, he knew that was the wrong decision to make. *I'll keep brushing her off until she gets the hint,* he figured.

"Not now, Corvette. I have a 10 o'clock appointment. I'll see you at lunchtime. And put some panties on. You're starting to scare me," Lamont snapped. "By the way, how many other men are you giving easy access to around this firm?"

"Mind your business," Corvette retorted. "Remember, you have a wife and children so no questions asked. Got that, mister?" She grabbed a handful of neatly stacked files and cradled them in her arm as if they were a baby. With her free arm on her hip she marched out of his office, slamming the door behind her. Her walk gave him quite a show to look at. *Damn! She knows she has a tush on her.*

Lamont kept wondering how he was going to bring this affair to a halt. *This chick is getting crazier and crazier. I know. I'll just bang it one more time then fire her freaky ass.*

Why do men think it's so easy to get rid of the other woman when they think with their head below their necks? Playing with women's emotions wasn't right and could lead to more than just hurt feelings. Lamont wanted to fulfill his sexual fantasy but didn't want to deal with the consequences. Shame on him for not realizing how precious his wife was to him – and to God.

Bzzz... Bzzz "Excuse me," Corvette said through the intercom. She was feeling kind of jealous because Lamont's client has been in his office for more than an hour.

"Yes, Ms. Corvette. Can I help you?" Lamont respectfully asked as he apologetically hunched his shoulders at his client who seemed agitated.

"Oh it's Ms. Corvette now, huh? When did you start calling me Ms. Corvette?" She tapped her fingers on her desk lightly, waiting for his comeback.

"Ahh... when I have a client sitting right here in front of me," Lamont said while thinking about how Corvette was tripping. He scratched his forehead and glanced back at his beautifully attractive client, Lisa Smith. *Damn, I could do her also,* he thought. Just like a typical male, Lamont didn't realize he was already about to drown.

"Ms. Corvette, I'll get back to you later. I have an important client I have to attend to at the moment, so I'll talk to you soon."

"Lamont...Lamont...if you hang up on me, I mean it, you'll pay. It's almost lunchtime and you've been in there with that bimbo for almost two hours."

Oh God! Did she really just call my client a bimbo? As soon as I'm finished I'll take care of her crazy ass. Lamont was appalled Corvette had the nerve to disrespect his client, but it would make firing her even easier. Donald Trump wasn't the only one who could say you're fired.

"Yes, I do have a lot of paperwork to look through," Corvette said. If the intercom could have felt the steam coming from Corvette's body it would have melted Lamont's desk. Corvette's anger had gotten the best of her.

"As a matter of fact can you look up this account? We're trying to figure out where $25,000 disappeared to."

"I'm not looking up squat," Corvette snapped.

"The sooner the better, please," Lamont said, softening his tone. Corvette's smiled so hard Lisa felt her dimples through the intercom.

He better had changed his mind. "Ok, what's the account number?" Corvette asked while pacing around her small office. Lamont said the number so fast she didn't have a chance to grab something to write it on but instead jotted it down on the palm of her hand.

"It's FT.*12778924*…Thanks so much, Ms. Corvette."

Here we go again with this Ms. Corvette shit. She pushed the button on the intercom and began her research.

"I apologize, Ms. Smith. My secretary can be overwhelming at times," Lamont lied. Lisa could smell a lie a mile away, and common sense told her something was probably going on between her attorney and his secretary. Nonetheless, she was there for one reason and one reason only, and that was an explanation about where her money was so she could proceed with her divorce.

"It's ok Mr. Trappe," she lied

"You don't have to call me Mr. Trappe. Just call me Lamont."

"No. I prefer to keep it strictly professional. I just want to find out where my money is, so if you can kindly find my $25,000 I'd really appreciate it and I'll be out of your way so you can have your lunch date." Lisa added that last bit just to see if Lamont would bite.

"Lunch time can wait. My client comes first." Lamont felt the vibes vibrating off of Mrs., soon-to-be-Ms., Lisa Smith's breast.

Lamont leaned over his desk and licked his client's breasts until her nipples hardened. Lisa allowed Lamont to taste her DKNY perfume as she slowly unbuttoned her blouse and he began drooling all over her small, firm breasts. *Let me lick you up and down until you say stop,* he hummed. Lisa couldn't resist anymore. She climbed on top of his desk, knocking everything off, and began performing oral sex on Lamont like nobody's business. When she finished, he inserted his manhood into her moist garden and began pumping harder than his pulse was racing.

Lamont took a second glimpse at Lisa and felt a mean streak coming from her. *I see she's not tolerating a half-stepping lawyer.* He knew it was time to stop daydreaming and get down to business.

"Now when is the last time you withdrew money from this account?" he asked.

"I've never taken money from this account. This is my own personal savings account. My husband, I mean soon-to-be ex-husband, knew about it but his name isn't on it."

"Oh, I see. Well there have been three withdrawals in a three-month span with your signature," Lamont said.

"I know, and every time I called to find out who made a withdrawal from my account the teller said I did."

"So it took three withdrawals before you came to ask me to search your account records? Lamont questioned.

"I've been out of town on a private business meeting, and I just returned to The City of Brotherly Love so I need to know what in the hell is going on with my damned money. We're in the middle of a messy ass divorce so what gave him the right to take my money?" Lisa stood and walked toward the windows to view the city.

"Because you're my lawyer I thought all of my accounts were frozen until after the final settlement."

"I'm sorry for the mishaps, Mrs. Smith."

"Just get on with my case," she said. "I want to be out of this marriage as quickly as possible."

Corvette peeked her head through the crack in the door before baby tapping on the wall trying to bust Lamont in action. She knew he had a habit of getting his way with women, and all Lisa had to do was be down with it and Lamont would dive in like Michael Phelps.

"Excuse me. Here's Mrs. Smith's account file with all of her transactions."

"Thank you, Ms. Corvette," he said jokingly. Corvette glanced at him with her game face on. *Don't make me mad.*

"With all due respect, Mrs. Smith, will you accept my deepest apology for calling you a bimbo?" Corvette asked disingenuously.

"It's fine. I'm used to home wreckers like you acting like you can't find a single man of your own," Lisa said. "Women like you feel good only when you're freaking with other women's husbands. So do yourself a favor and wait until I leave for your shenanigans."

Damn. Lisa is hard core. She put Corvette right in her place with quickness. Lamont was speechless. *Someone finally gave it to her besides me.*

"I need my job so I'll walk out this door like I never heard a word from your pathetic mouth," Corvette retorted. "And wives like you, if you took care of your husbands you wouldn't have to worry about home wreckers like me. Now isn't that right, *Mister*? Lamont was startled when Corvette put him on the spot like that.

This trick is so fired as soon as I find another secretary. Lamont thought about Corvette's friend Fancy since Corvette was the one who taught her the ropes. *Damn. Fancy works down the hall for my colleagues.*

"Hey, hey, okay ladies. That's enough. Thanks for the files," Lamont said sternly. "You may excuse yourself now."

"Me? Oh....ok...I see," Corvette said as she pointed in Lamont's direction.

The big time lawyer shook his head in disbelief over what had just occurred.

"Now where were we?" he said to Mrs. Smith as if nothing had happened just seconds before.

"My accounts, please," Lisa said, obviously angry.

Lamont placed the papers on the desk and they both leaned over to scan the withdrawals as if they were searching for hidden treasure.

"Right here it shows $5,000 withdrawn on March 9th, $10,000 on April 23rd and another $10,000 on May 7th. It's all right here in black and white – $25,000 total."

"I know what it says in black and white, but I'm right here in color telling you I need to find out how we can prove that this low life bastard stole from my account," Lisa yelled. She started pacing in her navy blue suit and white blouse. Her hair was pulled back in a bun, conjuring a strict school teacher who didn't take any mess.

"Find out where my money went and who forged my name," she demanded. "I want that person's ass in jail. We've been in this office way too long now, so during my next appointment I hope you have better answers for me. And watch your step before you're walking in my soon-to-be ex-husband's shoes. If you continue playing games with your shameless secretary you'll lose." Little did Lamont know Lisa was prophesying his future just like a fortune teller looking through a crystal ball.

Chapter 22

TRAPPE'S CHILDREN

Lynae was banging on Leona's bedroom door, having come home from school in rare form. "Mommy... mommy, open the door mommy," she yelled. Lynae was standing in front of the door in the middle of the hallway, hoping her mother heard her and opened the door. She tried the knob several times but it was locked. Lynae turned toward Kiya and shouted, "She's not opening the door." Kiya took off her Hannah Montana book bag and put it on the kitchen table. She tried persuading her little sister to let their mommy get some rest. Kiya explained to Lynae how tired their mother was after working hard at Legacy. Of course her words went in one ear and out the other. Lynae took a glimpse at Kiya like she was listening then proceeded to bang louder and harder on the door.

"Mommy, my teacher said you have to help me with my homework." Lynae screamed while waiting for the door to swing open.

"Girl calm down and come down these steps. Let mom rest. I'll help you with your homework," Kiya snapped at Lynae.

"No Kiya. My teacher said my parent had to help me with my homework, not my big sister."

Lynae was insistent about what her third-grade teacher told her. No matter what her big sister said, she wanted her mommy's help. Lynae threw her pink book bag down the steps then rolled on the floor having a temper tantrum. She repeatedly yelled she wanted her mommy.

Little sisters irk me. "Shut up Lynae. What did daddy tell you this morning before we left for school?" Kiya screamed. She had her hands on her tiny hips as if *she* was the mom. "He said she might be sleeping all afternoon, but afternoon is over Kiya," Lynae replied.

Kiya explained their mother worked in the casino and got very tired and would probably tell her about it when she was older. "So much goes on in that terrible place, and that's why she wants us to stay in school and get a better education. She doesn't want us to end up at Legacy."

Kiya told her little sister about a player her mom mentioned whose nose was running. Instead of him getting some tissue he wiped his nose with his hands. Lynae looked at Kiya like that was no big deal, which it really wasn't to a third grader. Kiya continued explaining that the snot transferred from the man to their mom, who had to touch the man's chips. "Ohh...that's nasty, Kiya," Lynae said, finally getting it.

Kiya tried cheering up Lynae by reminding her that their mom was on vacation for two, long weeks and they could finally spend family time together. "Isn't that wonderful? When Monty and daddy come home we can all play one of your favorite board games, Monopoly."

Lynae ignored everything Kiya had just said. Young children didn't understand work was mandatory. Leona always told them if God ever gave her a way out she would go for it. Being away from her children all of the time, especially on the weekends, really broke her heart.

"Mom.... Mom.... Mommy.... Mom?" Lynae continued banging on the door harder.

"Lynae, what did I say? Stop that now!" Kiya suggested they go play catch with the new ball Leona had bought for Lynae from the flea market, just until their dad and brother got home. Lynae paused and looked at the door. She realized the door was still locked then turned toward Kiya and asked whether their mom was dead.

Emphatically, Kiya replied "No!" But she remembered her father's words that morning before she and Lynae and Monty boarded the school bus.

Girls, your mommy has a headache and she probably will sleep longer than usual because she took some Advil's. I'm picking Monty up, so don't look for him to get off the bus. Kiya, keep a close eye on your little sister. Those words reassured Kiya until she had a sickening thought. *Oh My God, what if she took the Advil PMs that I put in the Advil bottle?*

"Come on Lynae. It'll be fun to play catch before doing your homework. Whatcha think?" Kiya finally convinced her sister to play. Most of the time older brothers or sisters could make their younger siblings do just about anything.

"Ok Kiya. I'll play for a little while then I want mommy, not you, to help me with my homework," Lynae said. Kiya agreed, telling her feisty little sister that soon their mommy would be well rested and ready to play with her.

"Come on, change your clothes so we can play catch," Kiya said. "Let's have some fun little sis."

"Okay Kiya, I'll race you. I bet I can change my clothes faster than you. And the last one to the porch is a rotten tooth," Lynae was obviously in a better state of mind now, but Kiya had never heard that one before. She often wondered about her little sister and what she picked up outside their home. *I heard of a rotten egg but a rotten tooth? Third graders!* Kiya smiled then walked slowly to her room in her smart and considerate plan to allow Lynae to be first one to the porch.

"Kiya, this ball is big. What was mommy thinking?

"This is a beach ball for when you go to the beach."

"Well, we're not on the beach. We're on the porch." Kiya threw the ball and it bounced off Lynae's head. *Why do 9-year-olds have to be so exact?* "Girl, just catch the ball. Daddy and Monty will be home in a minute." The girls played catch until sunset. Kiya reckoned her step-daddy forgot to pick up Monty once again. She had brought it to Leona's attention plenty of times. "Mom, why do you think daddy be late picking up Monty?" Leona explained that being a lawyer was an important job and sometimes he had to work overtime. Leona was lying, and Kiya knew it.

One night Kiya overheard them having a heated discussion.

"Lamont, I pray to God nothing ever happens to my son," Leona said.

"Leona, I'm sorry. I'll never be late again. I wouldn't forgive myself if something happened to my first born."

"Well, you'd better have your secretary do your late work and pick my son up on time from his practices."

A light bulb came on in Kiya's head as she turned the switch off in the bathroom. *My stepdad is cheating.* Kiya eased on back to her bedroom with the words of her mother ringing in her mind. *God will put your sins on BLAST sooner or later.*

Where's my dad? He's taking too long. Monty was really tired of his father picking him up late from practice.

"Hey Monty, do you need a ride home?" the man in the fitted cap shouted as his drove slowly pass the school bench.

"No, my dad should be here in a minute," Monty assured the white man smacking on his gum. "I'll just wait for him, but thanks."

"Ok, dude, but it's getting late."

"Yea, I know coach, but my dad told me to stay put." Minutes after the coach drove away, bad thoughts crept into young Monty's mind.

What if he got into a car accident or what if I should have taken the ride with Coach Rick? What if... What if...

Monty was starting to panic. Even though Lamont had been late before he'd never been this late. Monty watched the sun disappear and wondered how much longer he would have to wait.

"Hey...Monty?" Lamont said while creeping up behind him.

"Hey...dad! I didn't' even hear you ride up," Monty's frown became a smile.

"Boy, I called you three times but you were in a daze. What were you thinking about?

How was practice?" Lamont shot the questions to Monty all in one breath. Monty brushed away his thoughts and told him his dad he wasn't thinking about anything, but he feared his facial expression was giving him away.

"Dad, practice was great. I made two touchdowns today," Monty said while rubbing the grass stains on his left knee. No one could tackle me today. I ran yard after yard until it was touchdown baby!"

"Great, Monty. I hope you feel like that when you're playing against the other team. You know practice is practice but game time is show time," Lamont reminded him.

"Dad, I know I'm good no matter what. No other team can stop me. I'm number one!" Monty shouted.

"That's right. Keep encouraging yourself because confidence is key," Lamont said. For the rest of the ride home there was silence in the car. Monty was looking out the passenger side window still wondering why his dad was more than 45 minutes late. He just didn't have the courage to ask him. He was also thinking about the fact that his mother was on vacation, meaning they'd have a full house. Monty really missed his mother at night when she was working from 8 p.m. until. Kiya tried to substitute for her, and even though he loved his annoying, big sister and knew she loved him, too, no one could take his mother's place. He just wished he could spend more time with her.

Lamont drove very carefully trying to avoid getting another speeding ticket. He realized all the tickets he had gotten in the past had added up to a lot of money he could have spent on bills. Leona told him time after time they couldn't afford to waste money. He wanted to race home before he had to hear her preaching to him about picking Monty up late once again. He played his family role fairly well, but his inner soul was crying out. Lamont loved his wife but his wife, loved The Lord more than him, he believed. Lamont wanted more. He wanted to be held and loved at night. He reached to turn up the radio. *Power 99 FM* was playing Mary J. Blige's hit "All I Really Want is to Be Happy." Lamont tapped the steering wheel with his right hand while humming the lyrics all the way home. Father and son were in deep thought not knowing they were thinking similarly. Monty wanted to know why his dad was late *again* and Lamont was sorry he was late. *Corvette had struck again…*

Chapter 23

LEONA

L amont pressed down on the intercom and screamed into the speaker.

"Corvette, come into my office now!" *What the hell was she thinking?*

"Yes mister," she smirked while walking toward his office door.

"What the hell were you thinking?"

"Come again?" Corvette smirked again while starting to rub herself. She knew exactly what Lamont wanted, and then there was her big need. Even though Corvette had it all including a fancy car, nice house and money, and even though she successfully started a program for families in need, she was still missing love. Corvette's father chose not to be a part of her life, so throughout her life she sought love from other men – married men.

"That's not working today, Corvette. You really took it too far. You can feel all over your body all you want. I'm ready to call this affair off. You had no right calling Lisa a bimbo."

Corvette had never seen Lamont so upset. She knew he wasn't really calling it off but instead was just sounding like a broken record always saying the same 'ole line. *Corvette, it's over.* Once his wife came home tired and drained from work, not even thinking about breaking him off, he would be ready to get with her. Corvette knew it was only a matter of time before Lamont was giving it to her good again.

Lamont reminded Corvette Lisa was a very important client who was paying their salaries. He wanted her to understand the trouble she could have caused. "Lisa Smith is going through a very messy divorce, and it's our job to find out who forged her name on those withdrawal slips," Lamont said. He knew the husband had something to do with it; he just had to find evidence proving it.

"We can crack this case open, but if you keep acting like a hood ho in front of my clients I'll have to dismiss your ass. Do I make myself clear, Corvette?"

"Yes Mister," she responded in a low tone. "Mister, can you excuse me for a minute? I have a meeting in the ladies room and I'll be back real soon." Corvette smiled at him.

Lamont wondered why he snapped on her like that when he was the one who was wrong. The stress took over his emotions. When you play too many games at once you get tired. Lamont started balancing his hands up and down, as though he was weighing his options... *My wife and children verses my misbehaving, misfit secretary. Lord, I need your help. What have I gotten myself into? Two women. Three children. I'm supposed to be a man, a father and a husband. I'm not supposed to be fooling around. I have to leave Corvette alone once and for all. Today will be our grand finale. No more after today.* Lamont looked at the digital clock sitting on the corner of his desk and noticed his deep thoughts had him drifting away.

He wanted to know what was taking Corvette so long and felt a nervous shock in his belly. *I hope there will be no uproar after I break it off.* He figured after telling her he didn't want to be bothered with her anymore the hood rat in her might emerge. Men know how chicks can get when they stop giving them good loving, money or both. They start off like Dr. David Banner and end up like The Incredible Hulk. Lamont continued thinking about how he could break away from Corvette and start anew with his wife. Leona meant the world to him because even before he was somebody, a big shot attorney, she loved him.

Leona was with Lamont when he didn't have anything, and she used to always buy him Krispy Kreme donuts every other Friday to symbolize how sweet he was. The unbelievable love she made to him is what he missed the most. He knew he'd be a fool to get out of a lifelong marriage now. The fact of the matter was he needed to come clean and get right for his own sake.

Men always want to know why women have attitudes, but they should stop their unnecessary crap. Leona gave Lamont two beautiful children and stood her ground as a wife, a mother and a friend throughout their entire relationship without wavering once. The decision wasn't hard at all, Lamont thought. Not to mention after what he saw today he didn't know what to expect from Corvette anymore. All he needed to do was figure out how to get rid of her peacefully. Corvette already proved she could win an Oscar for her performance. Lamont wanted to go back to being a good husband and live up to the vows he took.

Lamont always blamed other women for his sick ways. He'd had plenty of affairs in his thoughts – like with his client, Lisa Smith – but never acted them out in the flesh until Corvette came to work for him. He always fantasized about doing his secretaries, but little did he know it would one day become a reality. Or should he say a nightmare.

Bzzzz… bzzzzz "Frisby and Trappe law firm. May I help you?" Lamont wondered why he was answering the phone. *Where is she? This is her damned job to answer the phones.*

"Hey Missster Big Daddy,"

"Girl, why are you calling me?" I thought you had to take care of something," an irritated Lamont said.

"Yes I did. I found out some information on Mrs. Smith's account"

"What? More information," Lamont said with a confused expression.

"Calm down. I'm fixing myself up and leaving the ladies room now with all of the information you need." Corvette folded the papers and put them between her double D's. I'll be there in a second, mister," she said. *I'll be damned. You're trying to be stingy with my package. If you do I'll go postal on that ass,* she thought to herself as she walked back to his office.

Fantastic! She found out some information and Lisa can finally stop calling. Lisa had called three times already since she left his office. Now Lamont could finally update her on the $25,000. Lamont knew in his mind and felt in his gut that Corvette Ford was one of the best damned secretaries in the firm – both for her intelligence and her sexiness. On the other hand she may be the worst mistake he ever made. *This has to come to an end. She may be cute but today I witnessed how ugly she could get, and it wasn't a good look.* For Lamont to be a-top-of-the-line attorney, he sure wasn't a top-of-the-line husband.

"Knock. Knock, can I come in?"

"You're already in," Lamont said.

"I know. I just wanted to start off with some small talk. What's been up with you? You've been acting strange all day."

"Nothing. I'm just tired of the games we play. It's time to cut the strings."

"What strings, Mister?"

"Corvette, don't play dumb with me," Lamont said. "I'm talking about our attachment. We can no longer do this. We have to put an end to this now, for once and for all.

He couldn't believe he got it all out without Corvette interrupting him. Corvette had a stunned look on her face, and Lamont started to panic. He saw the look in her eyes and feared she was about to go postal.

"Corvette, say something," he frantically demanded.

"Oh, I'm going to say something, a whole frigging mouth full. You see these papers I'm holding in my hand. Mrs. Smith will never know where her money disappeared to and your wife, yea your wife will know everything by tonight," Corvette said with a bounce in her voice. "I don't know what type of woman you think I am that you can just freak me then throw me away when you decide you're finished. If you think you can get rid of me that easily I'll have your ass living in a motel because I know your wife isn't going to have a sorry ass man lying up in her bed. You come to work and wax my ass all up and down your desk whenever you want, so just mess with me and watch who winds up the biggest winner and the biggest loser.

Before Lamont knew it Corvette had him up against his desk.

"Before we say good bye I'll leave you with this." Corvette took Lamont's erupt manhood in her mouth and tossed it every which way but loose.

"What are you doing to me?" Lamont groaned, knowing full well he was enjoying the unforgettable moment, not the mention the warmth of her jaw and gums.

"Shut up and enjoy it," she mumbled, so Lamont did exactly that.

Now look a here, Corvette thought. *For someone who wants to call it quits his pole is about as hard as a damned pipe.* Lamont allowed his manhood to control his emotions. Long clear, glazed semen dribbled from his manhood and Corvette continued licking the sweetness off of him.

"Cooorrr..........vvvette," Lamont moaned.

"That's right. Call my name, mister." Corvette stayed on her knees for 20 minutes and afterward patted herself on the back. A girl knows a man's weakness – good head. After her performance Lamont returned the favor and then the two bumped uglies.

"Corvette, your lips, your hips" Lamont whispered in her ear. Right when Lamont wanted to stop his orgasm became so strong it rushed from his head down to his feet and the tingling sensation went through his body making him forget all about his wife Leona and his son Monty. Lamont could go for hours once he was in the groove, and Corvette's game was tight.

"Turn around ho," Lamont said, smacking her backside. He enjoyed watching her tush shake like Jell-O.

"Yup mister I'm your ho and don't ever forget that." Corvette knew exactly what she was doing. Lamont bent Corvette over and slammed her head against Leona's picture. The glass broke and shattered across the desk; however, that didn't stop him from man-handling her. Lamont rammed his manhood inside Corvette as she meditated on the vibrating throbs. Her face was moving back and forth on his daily planner and her cheeks brushed from date to date on his calendar. She screamed something Lamont had never heard her say before.

"I love you Lamont. I love you...I looovvve yooooouuu daddy."

"You do, huh? So does that mean you're going to start listening to me?" he said.

"Yes missssssster, I am."

Lamont's Blackberry went off once again. This time he picked it up with his left hand as his right hand clutched Corvette's long, black hair. He looked to see another reminder on his phone that read PICK UP SON ATFER SCHOOL PRAC B-4 5:15. Now Lamont knew he was extra late. *DAMN... DAMN... DAMN! I'm late once again.* Lamont stopped and rushed to put on his clothes, leaving his tie on his chair.

"Wait. I didn't bust mine yet," Corvette shouted.

"Well baby you'll have to finish yourself because if I don't pick up my son my wife is going to bust me, and I'm already 15 minutes late." Lamont hurried as he tucked his damped buttoned-up shirt in his wrinkled pants. He ran out the door, leaving it wide open. Corvette stared in space while sitting on top of his desk. She felt and looked like she had just gotten dumped on the side of the road.

After Corvette got herself together and collected her thoughts about how she was going to tell his wife she questioned whether to confront her at home or on her job. She knew either way it was time to let her know what type of husband she had. *Lamont is a no good, low-down dirty wannabe old ass player. Yup. That sums it up.* She glanced at the mirror to fix her hair and noticed she was bleeding terribly.

"Help….. Help… Help…. HELP!" Her screams were in vain because Lamont was long gone. At that very moment she had an epiphany. She realized she didn't want to be second to anyone any longer. Her screams drifted down the hallway where Fancy was typing.

What…in the heck is going on? Fancy jumped up, knocking over all of the papers on her desk, and ran as fast as she could toward Lamont's office.

Lamont raced down the lanes to beat the traffic lights, hating that Philly had all one-way streets. He couldn't even turn on red, either. Oh how he wished he was still living in Jersey because a two-way lane sure would do him some good on a day like today. He thought about how sorry he was while driving to pick up his son. Now that he'd gotten his groove on, reality started setting back in. *When I married Leona it was for better or for worse. I've done the worse. Now it's time for me to do better.*

Chapter 24

SJHB

Danni, the co-owner of South Jersey House of Beauty, told her partner Rena she couldn't talk on the phone right now. She had to put a full hair weave in Monique's hair. While Rena was trying to release the customer from the phone another client was patiently waiting to get the dye removed from her hair. "Bajing is no joke," Danni told her client. "It's very harsh on your head."

Sasha was patiently waiting to get her hair washed by Samaya, the assistant, while listening to the shop gossip at the same time. *I can't believe women really go to bed with their makeup hiding their natural beauty from their husbands.* Sasha frowned her face at that conversation. *Like husbands don't know what their wives' features are after years of marriage,* she thought. *Women better get more confidence in themselves.*

"Come on Sasha. What are you getting done today?" Samaya asked while they walked back toward the sinks.

"Danni and Rena did a great job with the shop," Sasha said, insisting on chatting.

The shop looked like an open lounge, with hardwood floors and full-length mirrors. It even had a makeup room.

"Yea. It took them only four days to turn around this shop," Samaya replied.

Once Samaya finished washing Sasha's hair, Sasha couldn't help but wonder based on their last conversation how Samaya's baby girl was doing.

"She's good, but I'm still doing it alone." Sasha felt bad because there were a lot of single mothers doing it alone. Why did fathers think they could just walk off like that and not help the mothers? Of course, in due time God had the last and final say. Keep your head up, Samaya," Sasha said encouragingly. Samaya thanked Sasha, dried her hair and they walked back up front.

"Now what do you want done to all this thick hair." Rena asked Sasha. "You know, just the natural curl." Sasha wanted a style that would last because she knew she had Tamal's mother's funeral to attend in the morning, but she also wanted to go to Terri's Zumba class. "Ok. The usual it is." Rena started putting mousse in her hair and twisted it down to her scalp. Because Sasha's hair was so thick she had to stay under the dryer for an extra 30 minutes.

"South Jersey House of Beauty," Samaya sang as she answered the phone. She relayed the message to Danni that someone wanted a price quote for her hair.

"I can't do a consultation over the phone. They always want full assessments over the phone when they can just come in the shop and let me consult with them. You know what I mean Rena? Seeing the hair is important. I must actually see it before I give them a quote."

"I know what you mean, Danni, but they're your clients so you better let them know when they call."

Danni and Rena continued doing their clients' hair side by side. Sasha sat under the dryer and overheard a lady yelling on her cell phone. The brown-skinned woman was snapping on someone for not picking up her son from school and saying now he was missing. Ahh man, Sasha thought. After overhearing a few more calls Sasha felt relieved to know the woman had located her son.

"Come on, Sasha. Your hair is dried now," Rena said while taking out the Jheri Curl rollers at the end of Sasha's hair.

"Thank God because my ears felt like they were going to melt underneath that dryer," Sasha said.

"What time is Tamal's mom's funeral," Danni asked.

"The normal time, it's an 11 o'clock service."

"Yea, we were shocked to hear about his mom's passing. We used to have so much fun at Camden High School. Those were the days," Danni said.

"Yo Danni, remember when Tamal tried to hit on you in the cafeteria by asking if he could buy you lunch," Rena questioned.

"Right, but I was up on his bullshit ass. Girl, he was getting free lunch just like I was. Since then I knew he didn't have any game."

Brandy the secretary interrupted and called out the names of clients who had made appointments for the next day. She sounded like a teacher taking roll.

"Lisa."

"Oh she's good," Danni said.

"Kenyetta"

"She's good, too."

"Cheryl."

"Oh, I don't know what Cheryl you're talking about," Danni told Brandy, who simply continued with the list. She informed Danni everyone was getting washes and curls. Brandy swiveled around in her chair and turned toward Sasha. "Do you still stop pass Corrine's Soul Food Restaurant?"

Sasha had been going to Corrine's Soul Food for years and had been trying to get Brandy to check it out. "Girl, you still haven't gone there yet? Mrs. Corrine's food is good, but the encouraging words she always imparts are even better."

Rena finished spraying oil sheen on Sasha's hair and Sasha said goodbye to everyone as they waved bye to her. She headed back over the bridge without anyone knowing she'd been in Camden.

Chapter 25

PRIOR TO THE FUNERAL

E veryone was preparing for the late Mrs. Naydine Jackson's funeral. Even though Tamal had issues with women and a drinking problem, he still had a great support system, which everyone needed in a time of sorrow. Some people had to drive a long distance and some people had to walk only minutes to get to the church. It was raining hard in Philly and some drivers had to pull over because the rain clouded their vision. However, over the bridge in Camden a glow from the sun was shining on the church.

Ms. FORD:
Ms. Ford stepped out of her warm shower. Before catching the phone on its last ring she mumbled, *who can be calling me this time of morning?* She reached for the phone and noticed she'd already missed one call from her daughter Corvette. "Hello." The strange yet noticeable voice said. "Calm down. Hold on while I put my pants on." Ms. Ford was standing in the middle of her bedroom undressed. Once she was fully dressed except for her shoes she plopped down on her bed and continued listening to the voice on the other end. "Now what's happening? Hmmm, I see. Oh, I see son. Well after the funeral I'll give my manager a call if he doesn't call me first Thanks so much for the information." Ms. Ford hung up the phone and within seconds was deep in thought. *This can't be what's*

happening now. If it is I hope it doesn't affect me. I'm in a jam. I owe the IRS a lot of money in back taxes. How will I ever pay it all off? Suddenly, Ms. Ford bounced back like a rubber band, grabbed her suit jacket, rushed out of the house and jumped in her brand new *BMW*.

DAMON:

Man, should I go? Damon was contemplating whether he should go pay respects at his boy's mother's funeral. Damon had kicked it with Tamal only in the gym or in passing at bars. Not once did he ever realize the Mal he knew only as an acquaintance was Tamal, aka Mally, the man Sasha had to find so badly. Because Damon had lost his mom he knew the pain all too well. He decided to go. Damon wished more people had shown him love when his mom passed. For instance, his boys that he grew up with in north Philly or his aunt Crystal that thought she was born with silver spoons in her mouth. She just couldn't let go of her grudge against her sister, his mother, long enough to attend her funeral. Damon figured the least he could do was show his homey some brotherly love. Damon rose from his king-sized bed and started preparing himself for this sad day – not only for Tamal but also for him because of the memories of his mother.

BRENDA RUSTY:

"Oh that's nice to hear Fancy, but let me get off this phone before I burn these four pans of baked macaroni-n-cheese. You know they got me slaving like Mr. Belvedere. I'll talk to you when you get here, and I don't know why you're not bringing little man to pay his respects to his Granny Ma, but he's your son so you do what you want. Love you, too. Goodbye."

Brenda was in a hurry, but nonetheless she was in charge of the mac-n-cheese and the beverages. She felt providing a side dish and beverages was the least she could do for the late Naydine. After their big fallout back in the day she respected Naydine Jackson even more for wanting to be married with children. It was something she always dreamed of, but she never found the right man after she slept with the wrong man, which was someone else's husband. So she simply gave up on her dream of being happily married and raised Sasha, then her niece, Fancy, to the best of her ability.

Brenda removed her apron and went into her vanity to freshen her makeup. *It's almost time to say goodbye for the last time. Who would have ever thought Naydine Jackson, a sweetheart, would be going home to The Lord this early in her life? I guess God calls His people whenever He feels like it. Oh Naydine, who are you kidding? You just had to prove to me that Kevin Jackson belonged to you.* Brenda looked outside to see if any of the neighborhood boys were out so she could get some of them to help her carry the refreshments down the street to the church.

KRINA & TRINA:

"Hey sis, why aren't you going to pay 'ol boy's mom some respect? Trina asked.

"You know I'm not beating down the door to see Tamal after he dumped me for you. I don't care how long it has been. Don't get me wrong. Mrs. Jackson was a mighty woman and she kept me straight around the hood. And that's how I'll remember her. So I say you just go and pay respects for the both of us." Krina touched the side of her face and felt the slimy, thick and rugged skin.

"Besides, you know if I bumped into Sasha I'd have to pay that bitch back for fucking up the side of my face," Krina said while looking in the mirror to ensure her weave was long enough to cover her burn. "You know if it wasn't for Mrs. Jackson I'd have gotten revenge on that bitch a long time ago. Krina remembered Mrs. Jackson's words to her right after the fight: *She's like a daughter to me, Krina, so do me a favor and forgive and forget.* "But now that she's dead and gone I can whip that ass."

"Girl, please don't start a ruckus at his mom's funeral. At least wait until after we eat. You know Sasha's mom is cooking her banging mac-n-cheese, and I'll fight you myself if I don't get to eat some.

"Deal. I'll wait until after everything is over and then Sasha's ass belongs to me," Krina promised. The sisters agreed on that then continued eating their breakfast on this glorious sunny day in Camden.

CORVETTE:
Corvette really didn't like going to funerals, but Fancy begged her to join her for support. She had grown closer to Fancy but further away from Tamal since he and Fancy broke up. Corvette believed Tamal hadn't forgiven her for helping Fancy and his son move away from him. Little did she know Tamal had gotten his groove back and wasn't thinking about her. Anyway, Corvette reconsidered and promised to tell Tamal she was sorry for everything she ever did. Corvette left her complex to meet Fancy at Mrs. Greenwire's house. She tried calling her mom several times to see whether she was coming but got no answer. *She's probably getting super clean as if it was her funeral,* Corvette thought. She chuckled as she slipped into her black fitted dress. Once inside her red Corvette she glanced in the rear view mirror. *I wish these cuts could heal, but they don't look as bad as before…*

(J.T.) JOHN TROLLY:
WTF is going on at Legacy. All this bullshit is going down. I hope someone calls or texts me to tell me the rumor isn't true. J.T. jumped onto the Ben Franklin Bridge and just before entering Camden got caught in morning traffic. *Man, WTF. I'm trying to be on time for my main man's mom's funeral.* All J.T. could do was relax, enjoy the rain drops and listen to the oldies but goodies. He rocked his head to Marvin Gaye's classic "Let's Get it On." *I think my mom said she conceived me off this song.* He wanted to call Tamal for directions to the church but out of respect called Sasha instead.

FANCY:

"Come on baby. I have to drop you off at Mrs. Greenwire's house," Fancy told her son. She had decided not to allow him to attend his grandmother's funeral. She still had nightmares from her mother's funeral and didn't want to risk that happening to Baby T. She hoped letting him stay in Philly and get some good ole fashioned love from Mrs. Greenwire was the right thing to do. Fancy knew Mrs. Greenwire would have Baby T working like a slave and she'd teach him the ropes. *Thank God it's raining outside or she'd have my baby planting flowers. Open the door, pull out the chair, say please, say thank you, get up so your elders can sit down and give thanks to God.* Fancy figured leaving him with Mrs. Greenwire was a great idea, even though the rest of the family might be mad because they had never met Baby T. *But that's on his dad,* she thought. Fancy had considered driving through Camden a time or two in the past to visit her Aunt Brenda and the late Mrs. Naydine so they could meet her son, but she never did. *Tamal came in and out of his life, so since I'm the primary caregiver I make the final decisions.*

Fancy dropped Baby T off with Mrs. Greenwire before hopping into Corvette's car. Then she called her cousin, Sasha.

KYMBAH and KEVIN, JR:

Kymbah looked like the spitting image of the late Mrs. Jackson. She was 5'5", had straight black hair a little past her shoulders and an almond face with plump cheeks.

She and Kevin were sorting through Mrs. Jackson's things trying to find her life insurance policy. Kevin knew Naydine wasn't his biological mother, but he felt she had massive love for him. Kymbah wanted to find the policy so could give a copy to the funeral home director. Kevin wanted it to know how much he was entitled to according to Naydine's will.

"Dag. Where did mom leave her papers? Did you check all of her shoe boxes, Kym?

"Yea. I sure did." *Why is he so anxious for me to find my mom's insurance policy?*

There were many potential complications when someone died. Family members needed to know, in advance, where important documents were kept. Everyone needed to have his or her will and insurance policy in a safe place. It was also not a bad idea to share at least one copy with a trusted loved one. Funerals were stressful enough as it was.

"I know Momma Jackson left me a little something," Kevin said, as if he'd read Kymbah's thoughts from just a few seconds ago. "Truth be told, I, and not Tamal, was always there for her."

Kymbah cleared her throat.

"You were here only because *your mother* was unfit to take care of you when you were a child," she told him. "Now you think you're going to come up in here and prey over my momma's policy. Wait until I tell Tamal about this!"

"Calm down Kym. No need to get upset. I didn't mean it like that," Kevin, Jr. said while wrapping his scrawny arms around Kymbah. Then they both wept.

About 20 minutes later Kymbah and Kevin, Jr. were left with a big mess and a house to clean. "Come on. We have to pull ourselves together. We'll think about all this stuff after the funeral is over" Kevin, Jr. said.

"You right, Kev. I'm going to finishing getting dressed and I'll meet you at the church."

TASHAD and JANELLE:

"Babes, can you zip the back of my dress for me?" Janelle asked.

"I want to do more than zip it. How about I rip it off?" Tashad said as he pecked the back of her neck with a soft kiss.

"Babes, not right now. Tottie's in the other room."

"Well, it's not like he never heard us before," Tashad said.

"That's my point exactly. We need to calm down on the love making while he's home," Janelle said.

"So you're depriving your husband of some good loving," Tashad retorted.

"No. But we have to be a little more discreet about it. He's getting older, Tashad. We don't want him sneaking little hotties up in here do we?" Janelle asked.

"Ahh damn. Let my little man get some."

"Tashad Trader, how dare you say such a thing? He's only 7. Do you know I read in the paper the other day that a trifling mother allowed her 10-year-old daughter to have sex? Now the 10-year-old has a set of twins by a 12-year-old."

Back in the day children played double dutch, jacks , kickball, hop scotch, Mother may I?, 1-2-3 red light and other games. Those were indeed good times.

"Come here, girl. I'll talk with Little Tashad before he hits 12 and tell him to make sure he always straps up," Tashad said while grabbing her waist.

"Not funny, Shad. Now go up there and help your son with his tie so we can go pay our respects to our old neighborhood friends."

Janelle did a spin in the mirror and thought, rather conceitedly; *I see why Tashad wants to make love to me over and over. This body will make any man say hmmmm."*

Janelle had cinnamon brown skin that complemented her copper hair. She was 5'2" with shapely hips, full breasts and a solid, round backside. She wasn't as full figured as Fancy in high school, but over the years she gave her a run for her money. And she won the man – Tashad.

"Are you ready, babes?" she screamed from the living room loud enough for her voice to echo upstairs in Little Tottie's room.

"Yea. We're coming down now. Wait until you see my little man. Janelle's eyes brightened like she had just fallen in love all over again with Tashad Trader and her son, Little Tashad Trader aka Tottie. They both looked so handsome gliding down the stairways. At that very moment she was consumed by an erotic thought: *Tottie has to go to my mom's after the funeral because nothing's going to stop me from making love to the finest man on earth tonight.*

BRAZE and JOTT:
Braze's stress was eating her alive. She had been contemplating trying Zumba with Sasha but worried about how the other ladies would look at her because she weighed over 200 pounds. The only ones who seemed not to care about her weight were Jott and Ms. Ford, so she didn't mind fooling around with her. Jott was the father of her children and loved Braze dearly. Braze realized he loved her for her, just as she was.

Jott returned home to try to work on the relationship. He had found a full-time gig with benefits at the Laugh Barn just around the corner from Legacy casino. Jott and Braze spent the next week cuddling and doing all of the things they used to do in the beginning of their relationship.

Just because relationships get lengthy they don't have to go stale. Every now and then people should do something spontaneous for their loved ones. When people keep their significant others guessing in good, fun ways their relationships usually don't grow old.

"Are you ready, Braze? My sister will be here in 20 minutes."

"Yea, but I think I look a mess in all of this purple." Braze didn't *think* she looked a mess. She *knew* she did. She just wanted to get her fiancé's approval.

Damn baby! I love you, but with all of those extra pounds you could be an extra for Barney. "I love you Braze, but..." Jott's voice trailed off.

"What were you going to say after you said I love you, Jott?" Braze demanded to know.

"Nothing, baby. I'm just glad to be home, but I do think you need to change into something else. Why don't you wear your black suit?"

"I'm glad you said that because I felt like I was about to try out for a Barney episode," Braze said.

Jott nearly choked on his saliva. *Man. That's the same thing I was thinking.*

He knew better than to comment or nod his head in agreement.

"All right, babe. I'll meet you in the car. Black suit it is."

After slipping into her outfit Braze topped it off with a dab of Jlo. She rushed out the door passing her soon-to-be sister-in-law. If Braze wasn't mistaken she heard Jane say *it's about time you came to your senses.*

LEONA and LAMONT:

After all Leona had gone through on her vacation, a funeral was the last place she wanted to be. But now she was all for a homegoing. Leona prayed the preacher really loved Jesus and would bring the word so powerfully it would convict some sisters and brothers to change their lives. It was good to talk about the person and all he or she did, but Leona thought preachers giving eulogies should talk about what the living still had a chance to do. In Luke 9:60 Jesus said let the dead bury the dead. So she wanted to hear some living words. She hoped the preacher would tell the people they still had a chance to live for all eternity. She wanted him to tell them to stop playing with Jesus. After waking from the mystifying dream she had had, one in which a lot of craziness occurred, Leona knew it was time to write her book.

"Honey, do you think the children will be all right while we're over in Camden?" Leona asked.

"Leona, what are you worried for? Kiya watches them all the time" Lamont said.

"Yea, but we've never been out of town. My God, please keep a head of protection over them," Leona said, showing Lamont she wanted to ensure they would be all right.

"My God this. My God that. Come on Leona. Do you think if God was in this house you wouldn't have overdosed?"

"My God, like I said. And He's why I *didn't* overdose," Leona shot back. "How was I supposed to know Kiya put Advil *PMs* in the regular Advil bottle? Yes, my God saved me. He also allowed me to have a crazy dream and to envision the book I'm going to write. My God does not make mistakes. I want out of Legacy and he has given me hope."

Leona pulled her stockings up her long legs and stood in front of the full-length mirror. "Thanks to My God I'm still here, unlike some others, so that means he isn't finished with me yet."

Lamont was sitting in their comfortable chair in the upstairs den, like he had nowhere to go.

"I guess you're not coming with me to support my co-worker?"

"Look Leona, gimme' a break! I just don't feel like being bothered. I won't know anybody there," Lamont said, not a shred of concern in his voice.

"Wow. I plead the blood over this marriage right now in the name of Jesus."

Leona humbled herself and got down on her hands and knees. She prayed to Jesus to change Lamont's heart and mind, knowing we must give it to God and allow him to work miracles.

She brushed off her knees, pulled her jet black curly hair into a ponytail and put on a classy hat. If her hat could speak it would have said: *I'm all about my Father's Business, so step devil.*

Leona dressed classy like that every Sunday at church to ensure she was put together right for God. She figured if she got fly in Satan's world why not be super fly for the one who saved her life. She didn't care if people talked about her. They talked about Jesus and she didn't see any of them saving souls. Leona went downstairs and chatted with the children to inform them she would be putting in for a leave of absence from work to work on her book. They were excited and jumping for joy, and Leona was excited also but knew she had to take it one day at a time.

Leona turned around from giving the children hugs to see Lamont gliding down the stairway fully dressed, ready to support his wife at the funeral. *Wow, Jesus! You are the man,* she thought.

Leona smiled lovingly. "Thanks honey. I'm so grateful for your support on this day."

"It's all good," Lamont said. But to himself he thought *I still feel in my gut something's not right.*

They both grabbed their umbrellas and went out the door.

TAMAL.

I know I'm getting punished because I didn't forgive my pop or pay my last respects to him after he passed. That's why I didn't get a chance to say bye to my mom.

Tamal's heart was heavy, soaking in indescribable pain. He felt like he was a failure. How could he allow his inability to forgive, and alcohol, dictate how he conducted himself as a son and a father?

Tamal sat on his brown leather recliner for almost three hours before dragging himself up to get prepared for the most dreadful day of his life. He knew he was about to see people he hadn't seen in a long time, which he wasn't looking forward to. *Really. Who wants to reunite under these circumstances?*

Why couldn't people have a "Just Because" day and get together just because they liked each other and wanted to hang out with each other, he wondered. Tamal soaked his masculine body in the hot bubble bath, something he hadn't done in years. Normally it was the shower for him, but he couldn't believe he was about to head back to Camden, to the church he grew up in, to bury his mother. So in some ways taking a relaxing bath made sense.

Mrs. Naydine Jackson was and still is one of the finest, nicest women that lived in Ferry Station. Tamal knew it was time to roll out and head to Camden, so he put on the suit his mother sent him via UPS. The letter that came with it read:

Dear Tamal,

How have you been, baby? I got your address from Sasha. Please don't be mad at her. I just wanted to send you a little gift. Hopefully you'll wear it to your father's funeral. You know the funeral is next Saturday. That's why I had to hurry and send your package via UPS to make sure you received it in time. Son, your mother misses you, and I'm so sorry for what has happened in our Jackson household. Call me. I want my son back. Remember, God forgives and loves everyone, so don't beat up on yourself.

Tamal ripped the tags off the unnamed dark navy suit. He put on a white buttoned-up shirt with a striped navy blue and white tie. He knew in his heart his mother had forgiven him, which gave him some small comfort on this day. He glanced out the window and saw the rain, which he truly believed in his heart represented both his and his mother's tears. Not long after that he transformed into a smooth Godfather. He was on his way to pay his hometown a long overdue visit and give his mother the best goodbye kiss ever. *Mama, I'm sorry. Mama. I'm so sorry, he sobbed.*

SASHA:

Why does everyone keep calling me from the job? I'm not answering shit. Legacy won't see my black ass tonight. Sasha had already ignored three calls from her co-workers, so even though she didn't want to she thought she should take this one. To her relief, just as she answered she noticed the display window said Fancy.

"Hello. What's up cuz," Sasha said.

"Nothing. I just wanted to tell you your girl's husband has been doing some downright doggish shit to my homegirl," Fancy said. "You know, the lawyer."

"Look, I don't have time to play murder she wrote. So either you're going to spit it out or I'll see you at the funeral." Sasha heard a voice in the background saying go ahead, you can tell her everything.

"Tell me what," Sasha yelled, impatiently.

"Corvette just told me Lamont caused those cuts to her face."

"What cuts? You made me aware he's cheating and now you're telling me he's a wife beater also?"

"No! This happened during one their sex-charades," Fancy said.

"Well, I have better things to do, and I think you need to be more worried about yourself than someone else's business," Sasha snapped. *Like the fact that Tashad, and not Tamal, is your baby's father.*

"And what was that supposed to mean," Fancy asked, agitation in her voice.

"Nothing. I've got to go. I'll talk to you later." Sasha clicked over and J.T was on the other line. Sasha gave him directions to the church. (Right on Market Street. Turn left on 5th Street. Keep left at the fork and continue on 5th Street until you make a right on Ben Franklin Bridge. Take the Market Street exit, 5B, toward downtown Camden. Take the 1st left on Haddon Avenue. Turn right on Benson and the church will be on the left.)

Not a minute later after Sasha hung up the phone beeped again. *Who is it this time? Oh, it's my mother. Ugh.* Sasha knew if she didn't answer Brenda would keep calling until she saw her at the funeral, and she knew if she answered Brenda would talk to her until she arrived at the funeral. Either way, Sasha felt she was in a no-win situation.

"Hello mom."

"Hey baby. I thought you would have been down here already."

"No. I'm just getting dressed. I'll be there in an hour," Sasha said with annoyance in her voice.

"Hurry up. And Sasha," Brenda paused with fear.

"Yes, mother?"

"Now is the time to tell Tamal the truth. I think…"

"Why now mother? Sasha snapped. "Is it because both of his parents are dead and gone now and you think it's finally ok to tell my half-brother the naked truth about how you slept with his mother's husband and out came me? For 20-plus years you kept it from me and then after I learned I kept your nasty little secret *for you*. Wow, mom. Thanks for your permission. I'll see you when I get over the bridge. Don't hug me. I'll hug you."

Sasha hung up the phone feeling very angry. She had to calm herself down before heading over the bridge. She put her cell on silent and slithered into her black body dress that didn't miss any curves on her shapely body. She slipped into her red pumps, put on her Gucci shades, grabbed her umbrella and dashed out the door. *When it's time...When it's time Tamal will know everything.*

Fashionably late was an understatement for Sasha's arrival.

Chapter 26

FUNERAL

"*A*mazing Grace, how sweet the sound that saved a wretch like me...I once was lost but now I'm found. Was blind, but now, I see." Chennita's voice permeated the air. Braze squeezed her fiancé's hand as if she was releasing her sorrow for Tamal into him.

"It's okay, baby. Let it out. I know how you all feel about Tamal," Jott whispered into her ear.

Braze glanced to her left and saw Leona and Lamont sitting two rows down from her. She couldn't really tell how Leona was taking the hurt for Tamal. All she could see was the back of her hat and her head leaning on her husband, Lamont's, shoulder. *I'm telling you, Braze, God wants you and Jott to be a union. To keep living in sin is not healthy for you or your children.* Leona's voice and words were ringing in Braze's ears. *After all these years I don't see why you won't just marry the man. He proves over and over just how much he loves you. Yea, he might have lost his job, and I know he didn't really have a steady job after that but he has been there for you and the children like a man is supposed to be. Besides, 15 years are more than enough time to date without tying the knot.*

Suddenly Braze was no longer hearing Leona's voice in her ears but instead her own. *You know what, Leona, you're right. Because 15 years are long enough, and I can no longer live like I'm living.* Braze removed her hand from Jott as if she was about to clap.

After hearing pastor P.C. give encouragement to the congregation, instead of clapping she put her arms around Jott's neck, leaned over and whispered in his ear, "Yes. I will marry you."

"Babes, not right now. We can talk about this when we get home. We are here to pay our respects to your co-worker/friend." Jott politely released Braze's hands from around his neck. "Now pay attention to the pastor because he's preaching some good stuff." *Now how does he know what he's preaching given he was raised in a catholic school, a catholic home and a catholic neighborhood,* Braze wondered as she nodded her head and said, "fair, enough." Jott sensed her thoughts and responded to himself, *you're not the first African-American woman I've been with.* An interruption broke their thoughts.

"Excuse me, ma'm. Is anyone sitting here?" Braze looked up and couldn't believe her eyes. A response couldn't come from her mouth fast enough. "Ahh… ahh…"

"What's wrong honey?" Jott asked. "Tell the lady no one is sitting there."

"Excuse me, ma'm. My wife, well I mean soon-to-be wife is so overwhelmed with all of, you know," Jott said. The tall black woman in her three-piece dark blue pantsuit sat next to Braze.

"Everything will be ok," she said.

What the hell is going on? Excuse me, God. All kinds of thoughts were running through Braze's mind. *The church was huge and surely had enough seats. Why in the heck did she have to sit next to me? This is what I get for lying.*

On the right side of Braze sat her children's father, who happened to be an absolute sweetheart. On her left was Ms. Ford, her lover. Talk about being stuck in the middle.

"Naydine had gone home to be with The Lord. She was a mighty woman of God who stuck by her husband's side until his death. She knew her marriage wasn't perfect, but she knew God had sent her a husband for a good reason: to raise two beautiful children and a stepson. Naydine. Naydine. Naydine Oh, how we will dearly miss her. But God. Did you hear me church? But God. He brought us into this world and only He knows when it's our time to depart."

Pastor P.C. went up and down the aisle as if he was trying to get everyone's attention inside the crowded church.

Poor Tamal. I wish I could give him a big hug right now. Mrs. Nay was a mighty awesome woman, but she had some shit with her, too. Oh excuse me Lord. I know I'm in church, so I'm glad Leona didn't hear me. She would have given me the third degree. Sasha's thoughts were rambling, and she kept twisting and turning. The gray-haired lady asked her, "Are you all right, young lady?" Sasha gave her a two-second stare and remembered she was in a church. "Yes, ma'm. I just have to use the ladies room, and I don't want to disturb the row by getting up." Sasha responded more politely than usual. Now she regretted her decision to move down in the middle of the wooden benches so the couple could squeeze in with their children. "Ma'm." Sasha turned and looked toward the gray-haired lady. "Yes," she said. "You can walk out this way. We'll let you out," the gray-haired lady whispered. "Thanks," Sasha replied.

Sasha quickly removed herself from the pew. She glanced over and waved to Leona as she walked past her. She walked a little further and couldn't believe her eyes. *What the hell? Oh Lord, I did it again. But Lord, you have to excuse me this time. I know even you're wondering why Braze is sandwiched in between her two lovers. Damn! She should have been a star in 'Trapped Dealers' with all the drama she's about to encounter.* Sasha gave Braze the eye. *Ooooooooooooh Braze.* Braze knew what Sasha's eye meant. After a few minutes Braze joined Sasha in the ladies room.

Tashad and Janelle Trader walked in and sat in the back of the church. Sister Chennita and Shantel sang a Mary Mary duet.

You took everything I was and

Made me what I am.

And with all I am I worship you

"Sit *still,* son," Tashad whispered. Lil Tashad was wiggling as if he had ants in his pants. "But daddy, I can't. I have to pee pee."

Tashad's patience was very short when it came to Little Tashad. One time he made Lil Tashad hold his pee pee for two hours just to prove to him he could hold his urine when he had to. "What did I tell you before, Tottie? During funerals, weddings and school programs you wait until it's over before getting up. Now you sit there and you be still, too," he said discreetly in Lil Tashad's ear. Lil Tashad turned toward Janelle while holding the crotch of his tan khaki pants. "But mom, I can't hold it."

"Tottie, it looks like you're doing a good job holding it," Janelle said, jokingly. Then she leaned across Lil Tashad and whispered, "Honey, I'm taking Tottie to the men's room. I'll be right back." Tashad frowned. *This chick right here always gives him his way. He probably didn't even have to go. We shouldn't have brought the little stinker.* Tashad and Janelle both knew they had to come to support Tamal because of the passing of his mother, but of course it was hard to find a babysitter on beautiful Saturday in May. Trees were blowing, birds were chirping and people were shopping or partying. Who really wanted to watch someone else's children on a nice day like today? When push came to shove parents had to do what they had to do, so Tashad and Janelle had to bring Lil Tashad with them to the funeral.

Look what the wind blew in. Frisky Fancy. Damn, she still looks good even though she gained a few pounds. Tashad didn't mind that she'd gained a few pounds. He glimpsed at himself and reality kicked in because he wasn't the same 'ol muscular hunk that he was in high school, either.

Who is that she brought with her? Now damn, that's a brick house. I haven't seen anyone built like that in person, only in the movies. She's got everything fitting in the right places and going in the right direction.

Tashad looked at his watch and wondered what was taking Janelle so long. *Tottie must have had to do number two.* At that very moment Tashad didn't mind how long Janelle took because he was having a party all by his lonesome, fantasizing over the woman in red, Corvette.

Prior to coming into the church-

"Hurry up and get in the car, Corvette. We're already running late for the funeral," Fancy said. "I hate being the last one to walk in a church."

"Girl, who are you telling? It seems like all eyes are on me and whatever is being preached at that moment was intended for me as well." The ladies high-fived each other then Corvette leaned over and turned up the music. *Ain't no stopping us now. We're on the move.* The women were grooving and singing to the lyrics and sounding like they were at a karaoke club while speeding over the Ben Franklin Bridge.

"Damn. I can't find a parking spot." Fancy said while searching for an empty space. "Whoever built this church must not have scoped the land out first or either he just was plain crazy," Corvette said while looking for a space, too.

Fancy drove around the block searching for a parking space. "How you could build a big church like this with such a small parking lot is beyond me," she said, her frustration evident.

"Girl, as kids we asked the same question. My Aunt Brenda said he built it for people in walking distance." Fancy pointed to her left. "See around that corner are three sets of projects, villages or whatever title the white man gave them."

Corvette peeked at the apartments. *I hope the wake is not over there. I might have to tell Fancy I'll treat her to dinner when I chat with her later because I'm not project material.*

"That sounded fair. I guess this could be called a church for walking people," Corvette joked. Both ladies laughed as they walked two blocks to the church.

Can't touch this…..can't touch this… Fancy's ringtone permeated the air. "Now what does Mrs. Greenwire want?"

"Doesn't she have Baby Tamal?" Corvette asked.

"Yea, but for all she knew I could be in the funeral right now so why would she call my phone? I should have just brought Baby Tamal with me."

"Fancy, calm down. Something could have happened. Why *didn't* you bring Baby Tamal to his Granny Ma's funeral anyway?" Corvette asked.

"Because he's only 7 and I don't feel like dealing with his nightmares at night. It's not like his father was giving him 100 percent of his attention anyway, and he didn't really know his grandmother."

A few seconds later the ladies were at their destination. "We're here. We're at my childhood church, True Praze." Fancy opened the door and they walked in.

In the meantime Sasha and Braze were sitting on the bench near the restrooms.

"Now Braze, tell me how in the world and I mean how in *the world* you ended up sitting between your fiancé and your supervisor/lover. Please give it to me slow. You know I can't take it all in at one time, Sasha laughed.

"Girrrrrrrrrrl, I don't know what happened," Braze continued. "All I know is I was holding Jott's hand and listening to the pastor speak and suddenly something came over me and I leaned over and whispered into Jott's ear and told him I'd marry him.

"Well, did he ask to marry you?" Sasha raised her eyebrows as she removed a piece of hair from her face.

"Yes... I mean no.... Well yes," Braze replied, sounding confused.

"Which one is it?" Sasha asked. "Did he or didn't he?"

"Well, he had asked to me to marry him several times over the last 10 years but the last time he actually asked was a year ago," Braze said.

"So how in the hell, *excuse me again, Lord,* did you decide you wanted to marry him today?"

"Well, Sasha, like I said something came over me." Braze said as she wept in the palm of her hands.

"Hurry up and use the potty, and I'll be standing right out here," Janelle said. Sasha looked up from comforting Braze.

"Janelle Davis, I haven't seen you since God knows when"

"Sasha, it's Janelle Trader," Janelle said with a slight attitude in her voice.

"Oh, my bad. I forgot you're married now. By the way, how is Tashad?"

"He's doing mighty fine for himself. His music studio is coming along, and we've moved on up like The Jeffersons." Janelle sang as if Sasha had never seen one of the most popular shows in their day.

"Excuse me, where are my manners?" Sasha said. "Janelle, this is one of my best friends, Braze Carter, and Braze, this is Janelle Trader, an old high-school friend." The ladies greeted one another and remarked about meeting under such sad circumstances.

While they were exchanging pleasantries, a small voice interrupted them. "Mommy, my zipper's stuck," Little Tashad said. "Come over here so mommy can fix it." Janelle bent down and Sasha's eyes grew larger and larger.

"Janelle, this is your son?" Sasha asked.

"Yea, Sasha."

"By Tashad?" Sasha questioned.

"Yes. Who else would he be by? We've been together only since high school," Janelle said, reminding Sasha as if she didn't already know that. "We had a few minor break-ups here and there but nothing Janelle couldn't fix. You do see my ring, right?" Sasha nodded in agreement.

"Nice seeing you Sasha, and nice meeting you Braze. I gotta run. I know my husband is wondering where am I." Janelle grabbed Lil Tashad's hand and they walked back to their seats.

Braze and Sasha followed and went to their seats, but Sasha had lost hers so she sat next to a breathtakingly beautiful woman with scars on the left side of her cheek. She was so taken by the woman she didn't notice Fancy sitting on the other side of her.

"Hey cuz, how have you been?" Fancy said while reaching over Corvette's lap to give Sasha a peck on her cheek.

"Hey Fancy. Where is Baby Tamal?" Sasha was anxious to put Fancy's and Janelle's sons side by side. *Tamal, you are not the father* kept ringing in Sasha's head.

"I left him with Mrs. Greenwire because he couldn't handle all of this death stuff. I know this was his Granny and all, but he really didn't know her like that anyway," Fancy whispered. Then she nudged Corvette and asked whether she'd mind switching seats.

"Sure, why not."

"By the way, I'm your cousin's co-worker," Corvette said to Sasha, "and you must be the infamous Sasha. I've heard all about you."

There was that look again. If Sasha's eyes had gotten any larger she would have had to be rushed to the hospital with a bad case of too much information. If Sasha's memory served her correctly, this was the woman with whom Leona's husband was cheating with.

Sasha knew it wasn't a good thing to tell Leona because all she would do was preach her ear off. *You know Jesus has the last and final say so.* This was a time when Sasha knew she needed to keep her mouth shut. *If Leona's God is so good He'll reveal it to her like she expects him to do.*

Sasha leaned into Fancy's ear and asked "Is she the one?"

"Fancy gave Sasha the ssshhhh look and nodded her head up and down. Sasha's brain was running 100 miles per second. *In one day. No, not all in one day.* Sasha's mind went wild.

Pastor P.C. announced that if anyone wanted to ask Christ for forgiveness he or she should step right up to the altar. "Everyone needs to forgive and forget and let God handle your issues," the pastor said. At that moment Sasha passed out.

Leona was in her chair squealing as if she wanted to shout for joy. She kept her composure as she encouraged the middle-age charcoal fellow to walk to the altar. "Yes, Jesus forgives us all," Leona stood and shouted. Then she sat back down and rubbed Lamont's wedding band, but her focus was still on the altar.

Lamont felt uneasy coming to church, especially with his saved and Holy-Ghost-filled wife. He felt like every time he was in the house of The Lord the pastor was talking directly to him. Lamont entered the house of The Lord only on certain occasions, mainly when he had no choice. For example, if Leona had to speak he would show his support, and even then he felt like she was stepping on his toes. Leona reminded him all of the time that if what The Lord had her say convicted him, that was a matter he'd have to discuss with Jesus Christ.

Dear Brenda,
I understand if you never want to speak to me again, my love. I'm so
sorry we had to take a blood test, but you know Naydine wasn't
going to let me send you child support payments if Sasha wasn't my
daughter. I never meant to hurt you. If you can find it in your heart
to forgive me one day I sure would appreciate it, and the sooner the
better. I see Sasha hangs tough with Tamal. I wish I could tell them
they're brother and sister. I know as a man I shouldn't have stepped
out on Naydine, but the liquor had me going. I know that's not a
very good excuse, but it's the truth. I never should have walked down
the street intoxicated like that, and now I'm leaving you my last
little bit of savings and I'll be out of your and Sasha's lives forever –
just as you demanded.
Love,
Kevin Jackson, Sr.

"Get up off of me, Sasha. What the hell are you leaning on
me for?" Fancy asked while looking at Sasha and noticing her
eyes were barely open. "What, you didn't get any sleep?"
Sasha told her she didn't get any sleep because she was too
embarrassed to tell Fancy she'd passed out and was dreaming
about the letters she found – one from her and the other from
her dead father who was both a drunk and a man who
committed incest.

Fancy couldn't have possibly understood Sasha's pain,
hurt and grief – not to mention the lies she told, the deceit in
which she played a part or the anger she felt. So many things
were running through Sasha's head right at that second until
she would have given anything to be in Mrs. Naydine's shoes.
On the one hand she was dead, which wasn't good, but on the
other hand she wouldn't have to worry about the lies
anymore, the guilt anymore, the pain anymore or the shame

anymore. Sasha jumped up and made an exit to the ladies room to throw some water on her face. As she got up the pastor announced anyone wanting to make remarks about Mrs. Naydine Jackson should line up against the wall, and he insisted people limited their remarks to two minutes out of courtesy to the family.

Once Sasha made it to the restroom-area bench she and Braze had left just 25 minutes prior, she sat next to a woman with her head in her lap and a weave covering her face. Sasha touched the woman's shoulder. "It will be all right. She's in God's hands now."

Sasha thought maybe she could give comfort to someone because God knows she needed some comforting. What Sasha didn't know was she had touched the wrong shoulder, and after all she'd seen and heard at the funeral she was about to encounter a real jam.

"*Rusty Sasha, Rusty Sasha,*" the twin screamed in the coffee shoppe. *Sasha had a long line of customers waiting to order something hot to drink on this cold winter day, but after hearing her name yelled out, not to mention the way people mockingly said it in high school, she looked up and noticed it was Tamal's ex-chick, Krina. Now what in the world is she doing at my job?* Tamal had moved out of town, and Sasha speculated Krina wasn't there hoping to find out where he lived. Sasha poured the young Asian woman her black coffee. *"Not today,"* Sasha told Krina in a loud, clear voice. *"I have a long line of customers so whatever you want with me you'll have to wait until I get off at exactly 3:15 p.m."* Sasha continued waiting on her customers.

"No! We'll handle it now. You told Tamal to pick my sister over me because I have a baby and she doesn't. That's none of your damned business," Krina shouted as she moved closer to the side of the line that seemed to be growing longer and more impatient. Sasha was maneuvering slower than usual. *I have every right to be in Tamal's business because his father confirmed that when he and my mom had me,* she thought.

"*Look girl, Trina or Krina whichever one you are, I need you to be gone,*" Sasha yelled. "*I'm not leaving until you give me what I came for,*" Krina retorted.

Sasha addressed her next customer. "*Ms, you'd like one hot French vanilla with whipped cream with a drizzle of chocolate syrup, correct?*" The lady ignored Krina's screams and said "correct."

"*One French vanilla coming right up,*" Sasha announced.

Then, in the blink of an eye, Sasha had thrown the hot French vanilla coffee in Krina's face. Now Krina was screaming and frantically searching for paper towels or something which to wipe her face.

"You said you weren't leaving until you got what you came for, so I hope you enjoyed the French vanilla with whipped ass cream with a drizzle of hot syrup, ho," Sasha said to Krina.

"*Ms., that was mine,*" the woman said, acting as though she was oblivious to the fact that Sasha had just scalded a customer.

"*Oh shut up. I can make another one,*" Sasha snapped at the woman...

Once the lady rose from the bench and her face met Sasha's, Sasha realized it was Krina. She also noticed the brown dark burn marks made by the French vanilla coffee she'd thrown at her that day way back when at the coffee shoppe. *Remind me never to get burned with French vanilla, whipped cream and a drizzle of hot syrup,* Sasha thought. *The side of her face looks a hot mess.*

"Rusty Sasha, I've been looking for you and after all these years what a coincidence we meet here. Since I loved and adored Mrs. Nay to the fullest I decided to wait until after the funeral to get my revenge."

After everything Sasha had been through in the past hour it was virtually impossible for her to muster the will to fight right about now.

"Any day and anytime, Krina," Sasha said as she greeted J.T. coming out of the men's room.

"What's up, J.T. Why do you look like you just saw a ghost?"

"Man, Sasha, I just received this text while I was taking a leak. Go ahead and read it." J.T. shoved the phone toward Sasha, who hesitated to take it.

"Read it, Sasha."

"Did you wash your hands? I know how you dirty pissing brothers are. Shoot. Half of the women I work with don't even wash their nasty ass hands."

"Man, just look at the text I just got," J.T. yelled at her, his patience growing thin.

J.T. held the phone up close enough for Sasha to read it. [HEY J.T. DA LEGACY JUST DID A BIG LAY OFF. I WAS 1 OF THEM. GIVE UR BOI A HOLLA after the funeral, & giv Mally my condolences 1]

Ahh hell. What's going on today? First Mrs. Naydine dies, next Braze is sitting between her two sex partners. Janelle's son and Fancy's son look just alike. Tamal is not the father. After that I wind up sitting next to Corvette, who happens to be cheating with my dear friend's husband. I could have sworn I saw Damon. Tamal is my half-brother, which I have to tell him. Krina wants revenge. And last but not least our job just did a major layoff. What are Leona, Braze, Tamal and I going to do?

J.T and Krina walked off together leaving Sasha drifting in her thoughts. *Now how in the heck did J.T. meet Krina and he's supposed to be Tamal's friend and she's Tamal's ex? Well, I don't need anything else on my plate, so the hell with them. Besides, truth be told I'm glad she walked off with him because as emotionally spent as I am she probably would have whipped me good right about now. That, and how trifling would I be to get in a fight at the funeral of the woman whose husband my mom was cheating with? I'm the product of that affair, and poor Mrs. Naydine has been through enough.*

Sasha stood in the door entrance and noticed everybody was walking around to pay their last and final respects. She decided to remove herself from the church and glided out the big glass door. She leaned her head up against the side of the wall that read *TRUE PRAZE* is the best place to be. *I need help at this time, Lord. If you are a God to answer prayers I pray that you please make this day go away.* Later, Sasha continued praying in her car and prayed until everyone was ready to drive to the cemetery for the burial.

CONCLUSION

L eona was standing in the pulpit looking over her notes for the final time. She had a strong gift of speaking and encouraging people to walk on the right track, to walk with and trust in The Lord. Every now and then Pastor P.C. encouraged her to speak. Two weeks had passed since the layoffs at Legacy and the late Mrs. Naydine Jackson's funeral. Leona wanted to share her dream. She wanted to uplift the dealers' spirits, especially the ones that were involved in the layoff.

The church was packed. Even the people that still worked at Legacy came out to show support. Leona was grateful to have so much support and wanted them to know that greatness lied within. Leona's sister in Christ, Nycole P. Lyles-Belton, always spoke greatness into her life.

Ahem.....Ahem.....Can I have everyone's attention please? Before I get started I just want to say if you ever get a chance I encourage you to buy "30 Days to Greatness," an inspirational book by my sister in Christ, Dr. Nycole P. Lyles-Belton. She is known as a fireball, but I call her my *Powerball*. My sister is awesome, and the reason I'm speaking about Nycole in this way is there is always someone, somewhere near or far, who inspires us. She inspired me, and I thank God for using her in a mighty way. Now if you can all get on your feet I'd like to have prayer.

Everyone stood beside a few people in the back. Right before Leona bowed her head she saw Sasha running in, fashionably late as usual.

"Lets us pray. Father God, please help me today to do your will and speak your word in a way that blesses everyone under the sound of my voice. It's not about me, Father. It's about you. It's about your mercy and goodness and grace and the fact that we are all powerless without you. God, you know what's going on in this day and age, and I just need the right words to give your people to confirm to them that you are still the Almighty God. Let *me* decrease so *you* can increase in here tonight. I'm asking you to let the conviction land where it most needs to land. Father, we as a whole need to stand and be on one accord. Now please allow me to deliver your message with firm authority. In Jesus' name I pray. Amen."

Leona took the microphone off the stand and began looking toward the window. She saw two little Blue jays sitting peacefully on a branch and smiled because to her the birds confirmed she was doing the right thing.

"How is everyone today?" she asked. Everyone in the church shouted "fine" simultaneously, as if they were a choir in perfect unison. As Leona began speaking she noticed more dealers were arriving. The church was packed. The only way she recognized them as dealers was they still were in uniform. She assumed news traveled fast once word got out that she, a former dealer, was speaking today.

Three days after the funeral and the big layoff, Leona wanted to share the vision and dream God had given her. She spoke with Pastor P.C. and asked whether it would be ok and he was more than excited for her to speak.

"Leona, I always sensed you had the gift. Anytime you want to speak it's ok with me. My church door is always open for positive speaking," Pastor P.C. said. From that point Leona began writing and researching. Most importantly, she began fasting and praying. Even though she was nervous she did what God instructed her to do.

"The very first thing I want to say is thank you all for coming out and supporting me on my first day of a new life," Leona said. "God has given me some work to do. Number one is to write a book, which I started a week ago. Even though I got laid off from Legacy my life does not stop there. There is life after the casino, and I firmly believe that. Number two is I started a class to speak to soon-to-be dealers to inform them of exactly what to expect if they become casino dealers. I firmly believe it's so important to know what you're getting into. As a dealer you could easily watch your life pass you by, and I need them to know that."

Leona paused, took a sip of water and continued.

"My full name is Leona Janae Barker-Trappe, but in my dream I went by my first initial, middle name and maiden name only, or L. Janae Barker, for some reason. It was a very interesting dream to say the least. In my dream I tried to jump out a window, but my heel got caught on the ledge, thank God. Just as I almost hit the bottom my husband and the paramedics awakened me. You see, I had a very bad headache one morning and I took what I *thought* were Advil's only to later learn they were Advil PMs instead.

I was sick and tired of being sick and tired. I felt useless and helpless."

Leona paused again, taking a few seconds to gaze around the congregation.

"But now, thanks to Laurie D. Willis being willing to edit my book, and thanks to the encouraging support I received from others and most importantly thanks to me having the good sense to trust in God, and not man, I stand before you here today. I stand before you knowing I'll be okay financially, even though I've been laid off from Legacy where the working conditions were messy but the money more than paid the bills. I stand before you here today knowing I'm now dealing cards with winning potential far more lucrative than any Legacy jackpot. The cards I'm dealing now offer peace. The cards I'm dealing now offer grace. The cards I'm dealing now offer mercy. The cards I'm dealing now offer faith. The cards I'm dealing now offer hope. The cards I'm dealing now offer love. And the cards I'm dealing now offer eternal life."

Leona took another drink of water. The Holy Spirit was moving in her in a mighty way, she was delivering a most powerful message and most of the congregation was on their feet.

"My husband and my three lovely children are here with me today, and I cannot thank my husband enough for having my back during this very trying time in my life," Leona said. I would also like to thank Tamal, Braze and Sasha, my ex co-workers and three dearest buddies. Last but not least I'd like to thank Covenant Cookies for taking a flight from The ATL to be with me on this glorious day. God bless you, sister."

After the big uproar at the funeral two weeks ago Leona didn't know how she was going to pull off getting everyone back in the same building. She was overwhelmed by her new vision but knew God had even greater things in store for her. Preaching her trial sermon was a very important step. Leona knew she had been on the bottom of the porch for a long time and now it was time for her to climb the steps to greatness.

"I'm reading from the King James version, which my Grandma Smith always told me was the best. Please turn your bibles to Hebrews 13:4. Marriage is honorable in all, and the bed undefiled, but whoremongers and adulterers God will judge."

A lot of heads began turning and people started sucking on their teeth. Even Braze got a little uneasy, but Leona continued preaching.

"All I'm saying is God wants us to live right and live as one body in Christ. That means marriage, not fornication. It's not for me to say you're going to Heaven or Hell. But His word tells us we will all be judged. Fornication, shacking up or making up just to have sex isn't in His plan. When he asks us why we still live in sin what will we say? How will we answer? He doesn't want to hear it after we've had plenty of chances to come clean. Come clean right now. Get right with God today." Leona continued imploring people to live right for The Lord.

"See, I did a lot of dirt in my younger years, and I had my first child out of wedlock. Having a child so young, way before I was ready emotionally, physically or financially, brought so much drama and stress to a lot of lives. I asked God to forgive me and give me a second chance. He forgave me and blessed me to marry and have two more beautiful children. I see the difference between having a family and being a single mother. And trust me when I tell you there's a big difference. My husband Lamont has been good to me.

Sasha tried her best to see up front. Oh how she wished she'd been on time for a change so she could be sitting up front right now. She would have given just about anything to see Lamont's expression. *Oh Leona, wouldn't you like to know how he's banging my cousin Fancy's best friend, Corvette, right in his office? Oh well...* Sasha knew this wasn't the right place or time to dim the lights on Leona, so she sat back and listened to her preach.

"Now please turn to Ephesians 4:31-32. Let all bitterness and wrath, and anger and clamor and evil speaking be put away from you with all malice: And be ye kind one to another, tenderhearted, forgiving one another, even as God for Christ's sake hath forgiven us."

After Leona read that scripture the sanctuary looked up at her in disbelief. Whispers started erupting all over the church. *Who does she think she is? I know she's not talking to me!* Inside, Sasha's soul was screaming loudly.

"Settle down every one," Leona shouted over the microphone. She knew that scripture would hit home, so she wasn't surprised by the uproar. Still, this was God's house and through her He had more to say.

"Because we all have issues with forgiving people or being nice to people who aren't nice to us, I'm here to tell you to release that negativity and start anew with a fresh, positive attitude. Start working on yourself like I'm trying to work on myself. That's right. I'm standing here in this pulpit preaching to you, but just like you I have issues I need to work on, too. Just like you I need to get closer to God. Just like you I have problems. So I'm working on myself, my issues and my problems. And I guarantee you if you start working on yourself you'll feel better about yourself and you'll attract positive people in your life. Don't get stuck on where you are. Focus on where you want to be in the years to come. Work hard on it and trust God."

Leona told the congregation she had less than a wing and a prayer when she decided to write her book, "Ante Up," but she stepped out on faith and started writing it anyway.

"People, when you make accusations against one another it shows God only that you're in denial, feeling guilty or better yet just don't want to change your ways. Now please turn your bibles to 1Timothy 4:15. Meditate upon these things; give yourself wholly to them; that thy profiting may appear to all. All God wants you to do is trust and believe in Him. He can make a way out of no way for you, you and you."

The spirit had taken over Leona, and she leapt from the pulpit into the sanctuary while pointing her finger to demonstrate to the congregation that God truly loved them.

"I've been through some stuff, but when I look to the hills from whence cometh my help I know everything is going to be all right. Does anyone hear me? Do any of you have dreams or visions or hopes or ideas that you hope and pray will one day come true? Come on everybody. Don't speak all at once." Leona said that last line sarcastically because only one person had said amen. Nonetheless, that didn't stop the Holy Spirit from performing through her at that very moment, and convictions were heavy in True Praze that day.

Shalyn, the event hostess, maneuvered her way to the pulpit and grabbed the other microphone like she was the hype man at a rap concert.

"Praise Him everyone for He is so worthy," Shalyn shouted. She called Chennita to the altar and asked her to bless the
congregation with a beautiful song. Chennita was caught off
guard but proceeded doing The Lord's will while Leona
prayed with a few women in need.

"Praise the Lord, Praise the Lord," Chennita shouted as
her voice increased, seemingly making it hotter in the room.
Her sweet sounds of encouragement gave the church a different, even more loving feel.

*"Keep fighting, keep fasting, it's not over until God says it's
over,"* Chennita sang.

"What a beautiful song. If I didn't know any better I would
have thought sister Chennita wrote that song, but nobody
sings it better than Maurette Brown Clark," Leona said.

Then she continued preaching.

"Last but not least I just want you to turn your bibles to
Proverbs 16:3. Commit thy works unto The Lord, and thy
thoughts shall be established. With that being said, give it to
God and allow Him to work it out for you. When we are
hurting from something or somebody we can't do it all alone.
There are some people who are equipped to help you. I know
somebody, that knows somebody, and He is willing to help
everybody, if you will. In Romans 10:9 my God says If thou
confess with thou mouth The Lord Jesus, and believe with
thine heart that God hath raised him from the dead, thou shalt
be saved."

Leona looked around the congregation before finishing.

"I know this is a lot to take in at once, but you can come
down to the altar and dump your trash and let God dispose it
for you. Don't worry about what anybody says or thinks. This
is between you and God."

Just then Leona's eyes nearly popped out of her head
when she saw who had raised her hand, acknowledging she
was ready to let go and let God.

The woman began walking down the aisle in slow motion
as if she was a blushing bride walking to join hands with the

love of her life at the altar. While she was walking Leona started thanking and Praising God more loudly.

I really don't know why she's shouting and screaming as if I'm about to get saved and walk on holy water like her, the woman thought. *I wonder how she'll feel after I get finished saying what I have to say on that damned microphone she's spitting on.* Sasha had so many crazy thoughts running through her mind. She wondered should she let the secrets out of the bag or just shut up and let God work it all out. She continued walking and noticed some of the co-workers she used to cuss out all of the time. Then she saw her mom and Fancy nodding their approval and happiness over her decision to change her life, as they both wept heavy tears of joy. *What the hell? I wasn't that bad, was I?*

After what seemed like an eternity to Leona, Brenda Rusty, Fancy and especially Sasha, she finally reached the altar.

Would she really accept The Lord into her life as her personal savior, or would Sasha open her mouth and cause a whole lot of people a whole lot of heartache by revealing all of the many deep, dark secrets she knew?

The choir started singing...

DISCUSSION BOARD

Check Website @ vytaminvoyce2.com for contest rules

1. Name as many sitcoms hidden in the book as you can.

_____

_____

_____

2. Name all of the clues signaling that Leona was L. Janae Barker

_____

_____

_____

3. Name the five pages, by page number, that let readers know Barker was Dreaming?

_____

_____

4. How many Advil's did Leona take?

5. With whom did Fancy go to the prom?

6. How many baby's mommas does Tashad Trader have?

7. With whom did Sasha get into an argument in the break room and what was the argument about? (Be specific, please.)

_____

_____

_____

8. What is J.T.'s real name?

_____

_____

_____

9. How much was young buck bench pressing when Tamal tried to hang with him in the gym, and what excuse did Tamal use for not being able to hang with young buck?

_____

_____

_____

10. Name as many cliffhangers (or situations the book left unresolved) as you can.

_____

_____

_____

ABOUT THE AUTHOR

Vytamin Voyce is a 38-year-old mother of two from South Jersey, who for years aspired to write a book. "Ante Up!" is her first novel and is loosely based on her life experiences. Vytamin Voyce faced many challenges growing up; challenges that helped her become the strong, independent woman she is today. Her journey has been tough, at times, but she has continued walking down the path God set for her. Since accepting Jesus as her Lord and Savior, her life hasn't been the same. It is richer. It is more enjoyable. And her life's purpose is abundantly clear: Encourage and inspire others through books.

Although there were numerous times when she felt like putting down her pen and abandoning efforts to complete "Ante Up!" Vytamin Voyce has been blessed by the experience of writing this novel. It is her sincere and fervent hope that "Ante Up!" blesses everyone who reads it.